D0914625

SPOOK HOUSE

by M.C. Helldorfer

Bradbury Press
New York

Bradbury Press
An Affiliate of Macmillan, Inc.
866 Third Avenue, New York, NY 10022
Collier Macmillan Canada, Inc.

Printed and bound in the United States of America
First Edition
10 9 8 7 6 5 4 3 2 1

The text of this book is set in 12 point Caledonia.
Book design by Kim Hauck

LIBRARY OF CONGRESS CATALOGING-IN-PUBLICATION DATA

Helldorfer, Mary-Claire, date.
Spook house / by M. C. Helldorfer.—1st ed.   p.   cm.
Summary: Feeling lonely in his small Eastern Shore Maryland town,
twelve-year-old Will thinks he is going to dislike the boy and his
sister who move in next door, until the three of them band together
to turn an abandoned old mansion into a haunted house.
ISBN 0-02-743514-8
[1. Haunted houses—Fiction.   2. Eastern Shore (Md. and Va.)—
Fiction.   3. Friendship—Fiction.]   I. Title.
PZ7.H37418Sp   1989
[Fic]—dc19   89-30026   CIP   AC

For my sister, Liz.
Boo!

CONTENTS

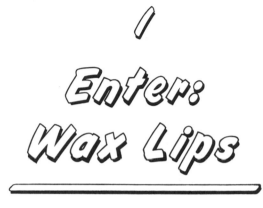

1
Enter: Wax Lips

TWELVE-YEAR-OLD WILL HANSON LEANED ON HIS broom handle to watch. If only the guys from school could see the performance next door. Jenko would make some wild joke about Pink MacDowell, and they'd double up like clams.

The new kid—"Wax Lips," "Rosebud"—was tacking across the grocery parking lot, his oversized rain poncho ballooning like a sail in shifting winds. He made his way slowly from a battered pickup to the produce stand, balancing boxes of fruit against his stomach, his chin, his puffy pink forehead.

From the diner's loading dock Will could see that the top carton was open, dozens of ripe berries

1

rolling inside. He waited, hoping for the right moment. His neighbor tottered on the edge of a pothole turned pond.

"Strawberry! Strawberry!"

The boy shifted his tall stack to look at Will. Box tumbled over box. Strawberries leaped from the cartons as they struck the ground. It was a beautiful sight: the caped kid doing a rain dance, trying to save the splashing fruit.

Will hollered into the kitchen, "Winston, come see."

"Can't."

"But you're missing something." Will was turning to argue the cook away from the griddle when he felt a stinging wet spot on the back of his neck. He spun around.

Splat!

Lucky, Will thought—then ducked. Near miss. The boy whipped off his raincoat and reared back again. Two more berries—bull's-eye!

Will dropped his broom and charged down the steps and across the adjoining parking lots. Seeing his neighbor dig into a fresh box, he raced forward to do the same.

Fists came up full. Bodies slammed together, locked. Handfuls of red fruit were smashed on Will's head, oozed down his neck. He wiped the pulp on the kid's shirt.

A carton got caught between the boys' legs. Falling sideways, they rolled in fruit and sand, into the lake of berries and out again.

Up on one knee, Will pinned the boy to the ground and was about to feed him a fistful of strawberries when he felt a strong hand grasp his own shirt collar. He wrenched around.

"You'd hit a girl?" She loosened her grip, but kept her shoe pressed against his.

Will took a breath and sized up the black-haired girl. Tall—an inch taller than himself. "I'd hit anyone who asked for it."

"Well, I don't hit boys."

Will glanced down at Wax Lips, who raised his eyebrows, then quickly looked away.

"But I smash bullies." Faster than Will, she scooped up berries. Her hand brushed his face as a screen door slammed.

The girl froze and Will glanced to the left, determined not to move his head. Scowling, the girl dropped her hand. "Mother is going to make you pay for these," she said as she let the ripe fruit slip through her fingers.

The boy in the berry pool sat up and looked Will over. "It was worth it." To his sister he added, "And I won't need another loan, Toes, so forget it."

"I will. She won't."

The woman, who walked with her arms swinging

a little, stopped at the borderline between the two parking lots and surveyed the tide of strawberries. "We'll discuss this inside," she told Toes and her brother.

Toes followed her mother, walking with long strides. The boy waited a moment, then reached down for a handful of fresh berries. Instinctively Will sidestepped, but the kid moved on, stuffing them in his mouth.

Will stared after him, shaking his head, then sprinted across the lot behind the restaurant to the Hansons' bayside trailer home. As he passed the diner's windows, he glanced up. Had anyone seen him? His parents were probably busy with the Memorial weekend crowd, the new waitresses all aflutter with Paradise's first wave of tourists. He could count on the cooks for silence, he thought, though lately he had felt Winston looking at him— through him—in a way that made him uncomfortable.

He glanced around for Digger. Hopefully, his dog would not decide to return early from one of his mainland hunting trips. The golden retriever had a way of wallowing in anything that was difficult to wash off.

At the trailer Will scrubbed his pink skin and combed the berry juice from his straight brown hair. He quickly changed clothes and, intending to wash them later, stuffed the stained shirt and pants into a crab trap and lowered it off the Hansons' dock. Racing back to the diner, Will took the kitchen steps two at a time, snatched up an empty tub, and pushed through swinging silver doors.

He was wiping clean the large center booth when Mr. Dan, an old friend of his father, squeezed by to take a seat at that table. "So tell me now, young Bill—"

The real estate man huffed between words, squeaking his way across the plastic bench. Councilman Barnes followed. Henry Wyeth swung in on the other side and winked at Will.

"Tell us all, just what kind of animal you trying to catch in that peeler trap of yours?"

"His father," replied a deeper voice.

Will looked back uneasily at the tall man in an apron who was pouring coffee at the counter behind him.

"Your waitress will be with you in a minute," Mr. Hanson said to the couple he was serving. "Now, William, isn't there something we need to talk about?"

It seemed to Will that his father did most of the talking. Standing by the toast machine, aware of his father's friends smiling in at them every time the kitchen doors opened, Will listened, shifting his weight from foot to foot, waiting for his sentence. The teenage dishwashers had stopped arguing over the pitching change in the Oriole game and were performing their task like perfect mechanical men. The waitresses, he noticed, called in their orders almost too softly to hear.

"And bus extra hours Friday evening, helping with carryout, and when school is over— Are you listening to me?"

Will opened and closed his fingers, studying the way his still-pink skin stuck together and pulled apart.

"I said no cards with Winston and the fellows."

Will glanced up at the cooks, who all looked away at the same time.

"And when you have apologized—"

"What?"

"I haven't raised my voice, William, and it seems to me I have more reason than you."

"But you said—Mom said—I remember, back in February when Mr. Dan told us who bought Randy's place, you said 'City people!' Just like that." Will imitated the drop of his father's voice. "'City people, moving in every day now, taking over, running us out of business!' That's what you said. And Mom said"—Will leaned forward, talking with his eyes, the way Mrs. Hanson did—"'They have children, Bill. Maybe they're a decent working family. Maybe they'll live over the store and keep the place up.' But you said, 'Barbara—'" Will knew he was a good mimic; he eyed the cooks, then rubbed his hand over the back of his neck as his father often did. One of the dishwashers snickered. "You said, 'Barbara—'"

"Maybe I should go over and apologize for the way we've raised our son," Mr. Hanson interrupted.

Will dropped his hand to his side.

"Either you go, or I will," his father continued.

"Going, sir."

When he reached the back door, Mr. Hanson called across the kitchen, "Ask Mr. MacDowell to write down what we owe."

Will turned back quickly. Don't you trust me? he wanted to shout. "Yes, sir," he replied, and trudged over to the grocery.

On the way he paused to look at the drying pool of strawberries. Glistening black flies picnicked on the bright red pulp. If Randy were here, Will thought, his camera would be clicking a hundred times a minute. His next-door neighbor had always taken a lot of pictures of whatever he found interesting—boardwalk lights, Polynesian Miniature Golf, Will and Digger.

But now Randy was snapping pictures 140 miles

west of Paradise, in Washington, D.C. Will looked up at the bedroom window that had once belonged to his best friend. He was probably using some fancy camera his new father had bought him, taking pictures twenty-four hours a day.

No longer a stock boy in a grocery, Randy was probably enjoying himself so much that he never thought about what Will had inherited: a city kid who, visiting school one day last winter, answered correctly every question Will's teacher asked him. Yesterday the new boy had hung a wind sock from the steps that ran up the side of the grocery, like some kind of conqueror's flag, Will thought.

As he entered the store, Will ran into Rosebud coming out. "I apologize," he said to the boy's back and kept walking. He spotted Mrs. MacDowell at the cash register. "I apologize." He spoke quietly, and before she glanced up, he turned down an aisle. There, banging soup cans with a pricer, was the girl called Toes. "I apologize," he told her as he passed.

"And you mean it, I can tell," she hollered after him.

He was glad she had noticed. Now, as soon as he found the kid's father, the trial would be over.

Will wasn't sure what the man looked like, for while his family had come with the moving truck the middle of last week, Mr. MacDowell had driven in Friday to open the store for holiday business.

8

A broad-backed man stood behind the fish counter. His hands were big, pink shovels, chapped, Will surmised, from years of ice chips and shelling frozen shrimp. At least the MacDowells hadn't hired city folk.

"Can I help you, son?"

"I'm looking for Mr. MacDowell."

"Well, now you're looking *at* him. What can I do for you?"

"I . . . uh, that is, my father sent me over here to apologize."

"You must be the Hanson boy."

"While I'm here, I'm supposed to find out what I cost you in berries."

"Might I ask your first name?"

"Will, sir. William."

"You like to be called Will?"

"Yes, sir."

"Sam likes to be called Sam."

Will fingered chips of ice. The dead fish eyed him accusingly.

"Loretta Rose, on the other hand, prefers to be called Toes. I'll never figure it out."

Will looked up. A patch of yellow hair grew high up on the man's head. His face was wide, genial.

"I wonder," said Mr. MacDowell, "if you could tell me why the boys around here call Sam 'Rosebud,' 'Wax Lips,' 'Strawberries'—"

9

Because he's got them, Will thought, and felt himself starting to smile. He stiffened his mouth.

"I mean, besides the fact he's got them," said Mr. MacDowell. "Sam looks like me, you know. When I was younger, smaller, and had a little more hair on top, all I was missing was a pair of painted wings."

Will grinned.

"But there's more to it than that, isn't there?" the man probed. "Is it because he's new?"

"Sort of. He's city," Will blurted. "And city people, especially the smart ones, can't be trusted."

"Can you explain that to me? City people, after all, are how Paradise makes its money."

Will hesitated. If his parents heard about this conversation, he'd be bussing every afternoon and evening in June. But he blamed them for putting him in this position, and besides, half the story was already out. . . .

"City people have bought up family restaurants," he told the man, "our guesthouses and hotels. They've started chains and fast-food places, which take away our business. They've built past the dune line, and that erodes the beach. They put up billboards, and litter all over the beach. They're building condos on the wetlands, polluting the bay, destroying the ecology, and we don't have the money or laws to stop them." Will ran out of breath in the same place his father always did. "I guess none of the grown-ups around here will tell you that to your face," he said bitterly, "but they're thinking it, and they're saying it behind your back."

"I appreciate your honesty," replied Mr. MacDowell.

Will felt ashamed.

"And in fact, I guessed as much." He sighed. "Well, neighbor, you don't owe me anything. I've made Sam responsible for the whole cost. If you want to work something out with him, fine."

Will glanced toward the front door.

"He should be out there cleaning up," the grocer said, stretching out his hand. "I hope we'll see you again in here."

2

STANDING SEVERAL FEET BEHIND SAM, WILL WATCHED the boy shovel strawberries and sand into a large plastic bag.

"Do you want something?" Sam asked, glancing over his shoulder.

"How much did this cost you?"

Batting open the top of the bag with the end of his shovel, Sam looked in. "It's a shame to waste it," he said quietly.

Will stepped closer, curious.

"You'd think it'd be good for something," he continued.

"Like what?"

"I don't know. But if it set a few more hours, I'm

sure it would attract some kind of interesting—"

"Digger," Will muttered, then backed away from the buzzing bag.

"Who?"

"My dog. You seen him?" Will scanned the adjoining lots. The MacDowells' pet, a small, hairy mongrel, slept on the grocery steps. Hardly a dog, Will thought.

"I saw him Friday, carrying a fish across the parking lot," Sam replied as he scraped then lifted a gritty shovelful. "Looked like a flounder."

"Been to the market again," Will mumbled.

"He shops for you?"

Will stared hard at the boy, then flicked his hands to make the boy look back. "So. How much?"

"Our dog's name is Schaefer. Twenty-five bucks."

"Tomorrow I'll bring you twelve-fifty."

Sam nodded and continued shoveling. Will had hoped his neighbor would act more appreciative.

"I guess I should help you clean this up."

"It's pretty well done."

The kid never looked him in the eye, Will noted, except when he was drilling him with berries.

"Blood. . ."—Sam spoke softly, peering into the bag—"There's been a murder, Inspector." He pulled a wire from his pocket and twisted it around the bag's mouth.

Will would have liked another look.

"So where's the market?" the boy asked, heaving the bag over his shoulder.

"Across the bridge, at the west harbor, just below—"

"Hey, Will! Willie! Yo!"

The shouts accompanied a squad of bikes that turned into the diner lot.

"Below the marina," he finished quickly, and started toward his friends.

"Near the May Estate?" Sam raised his voice.

Glancing over his shoulder, Will gave a short nod.

"How's the kid know about the May house?" Jenko asked as he and the other three boys jumped off their bicycles.

Will shrugged.

Jenko hollered across the lot. "Don't go there, kid. It's spooky. Don't go without your mother."

Al snorted and Neal laughed uncomfortably. Ray gazed for a moment at the blushing Sam, then bent over to fasten his bike lock.

"What's cooking, Willie-boy?" said Al as they entered the diner. "Who's cooking? Not you. You aren't wearing your apron today."

"Tomorrow."

Al was Will's least favorite person in the group. As a seventh-grade repeater, the boy had skillfully guided the others through a year with Ms. Kilborn.

14

Will was grateful for that, but tired of his know-it-all attitude.

"I hope something's cooking. This man is starving," Jenko said, thrusting out his chest, running his hands down his ribs.

Al and Ray greeted Will's mother, then Ray pointed to Jenko. "Do you have something to feed this man?"

"We might." She smiled at them. "Hello, Neal."

The thin-faced boy nodded to her, keeping his eyes on the rotating dessert case.

Will led his friends to the counter, then stepped behind it to fill four water glasses, which the boys immediately drained. Ray asked about the special, and the boys ordered the same thing as always. When Will returned with four cheese steaks and fries, they were talking about the fate of the old May house.

"My father's on the committee," Ray was saying, "as union representative."

"If they level that place," Al announced loudly, "it's good-bye fishwives, hello Condo-ladies."

Mrs. Hanson, who was passing by with a party of four, rolled her eyes.

"My father says if they build a condominium it will drive up dock rentals," Ray continued, "putting all the small fisheries out of business."

"Beating old Wyeth to the punch," Al said, glancing over his shoulder. "We don't need a union to tell us that!"

Ray kept his voice low. "Mr. Wyeth is buying up small businesses, which is different than putting them out of business. He's not taking away jobs."

"And he's not destroying the wetlands." Neal's voice squeaked a little.

Al looked upward as if he were trying to remember what his father would say next. "Yet."

"The bummer is they're going to tear down the house." Jenko bent close to Will. "This morning we rode by and saw bulldozer tracks all the way up the road."

"Nothing touched?" Will asked.

"Not a stick."

"What stopped them?"

"The committee," replied Ray.

"A court order, I think," said Neal.

"The people who care passionately about Paradise," asserted Councilman Barnes, rising up from the center booth. "The people of Paradise are not going to sit back and let big business types come in and ruin our beautiful natural habitat."

Will looked past the man, through the rain-spotted diner windows. A cinder block crab house, Fatty's Sub and Pizza, and the Pink Flamingo Motel

16

flashed red and green signs: EAT, EAT, NO VACANCY. Beyond Route A was another street of hotels, lots, and dumpsters, then the boardwalk, a narrow strip of beach, and the Atlantic Ocean.

"Do you know whether the person who bought the place is an outsider?" he heard Ray ask the councilman.

"I believe . . . uh . . . a company purchased it."

"My dad says we have to be more tolerant and—" Seeing the expressions on faces around him, Neal swallowed the rest of his sentence.

"Yes, well, your dad's a school principal," Mr. Dan called from the booth.

Mr. Wyeth wiped his mouth and grinned.

Jenko pulled Will's head close to him. "We're going to lose the house, old buddy," he said in a husky voice. "You hear what I'm saying? Before we even have a chance to get some girls there." He shook his head, and Will's. "Why couldn't they wait till we're married? We're going to lose the house."

Will stepped back. He didn't have to close his eyes to picture the abandoned home: a wooden, cube-shaped structure, a big gray block sunk into the marshy ground, more in front than in back, which made it appear to be falling on its face. Its porches pitched like a yawing boat and its shutters, nailed down seasonally by county officers, contin-

17

ually loosened themselves, swinging away from the dark windows. Haunted, everyone said.

Will liked to believe it. And though he had only some of Jenko's enthusiasm for girls, the house was just as important to him. Getting to the second floor in the stairless structure, making it all the way to the cupola at the top, was a dream he and Randy had shared. A hundred times they had tried to figure a way. Now, before his old friend came back for a visit and they had one more chance at it, the place would be demolished.

Someone was signaling to Will, for more water, he guessed, or coffee or catsup. Ignoring the summons, he continued to gaze out the diner's front windows, thinking of Randy and their plans.

As he stared he saw Digger loping along the other side of Route A. He lost him for a moment in the traffic, then watched his pet trot between cars that were stopped for a red light. Just as the dog reached the diner lot entrance, the light changed and a white car cut in front of another, turning suddenly toward the restaurant. Brakes screeched.

"Digger!"

People were in the way. Will couldn't see. He fought his way out of the crowded diner. "Digger!"

Another car back-ended the white one. The man driving the first vehicle had jumped out and was

18

leaning over the dog when Will approached. Straightening up suddenly, pulling his windbreaker close around his face, he leaped back into the driver's seat and sped off.

Will stared after him in disbelief. He felt people jostling him, a crowd growing behind him. Dropping to his knees, he buried his face in the heavy fur of Digger's neck. After some time, his father gently pulled him away from the lifeless dog.

3

Will by Himself

A POLICE OFFICER CAME, ONE OF THE SUMMER hirees, dispatched to his first assignment and very concerned about choosing the right report code for a rear-end collision caused by an animal.

"But Digger didn't cause it," Will insisted. "The white car turned on him, turned into Digger."

Mr. Dan pushed his way to the front of the crowd. "You're saying someone tried to hit Digger on purpose?"

"That's how it looked," Will replied.

"To him." Mr. Wyeth spoke quietly.

"Right," said the young policeman. "Anyone get the tag number?"

No one had, for the back plate of the car had been too muddy to read.

Will leaned over and removed Digger's collar, gently, as if the dog could still feel his fingers. His father began to argue with the policeman about the right to bury the dog on their own property. Slipping out from under his father's hand, Will walked slowly toward the diner entrance, curling and uncurling the cracked red leather.

"It's missing its tag," said Ray, who was waiting for Will in the middle of the lot.

"Yeah."

"I'm awful sorry about the accident."

Will shrugged and glanced away.

"We're all sorry." Ray spoke a little louder.

The other three boys, who were sitting on their bikes a distance away, nodded uncomfortably.

"We got to go," Al called.

"I wish you could come with us," said Ray. "Do you think, maybe this afternoon, your father would let—?"

"I have to work now."

"Sure. Sure. I understand." The boy climbed on his bike.

As his friends rode away, Will looked back over his shoulder. His father was still gesturing at the policeman. On the grocery steps Toes sat picture

21

still, both arms wrapped around the MacDowell dog. Will backed up and, turning suddenly toward the diner, came face-to-face with Sam.

"What do you want?" he growled. He saw his mother watching him, craning her head to look past the patrons lined up at the cash register.

"I feel real bad for you," the boy said.

"Well, I don't need you to, all right? I don't need you to."

"Do anyway," Sam replied, looking back at him with red eyes.

"Oh, give me a break," Will muttered, and rushed away to the trailer, where he could cry alone.

It wasn't the first night Will had spent without Digger, but it was the first time he had lain in bed without being able to imagine what mischief his dog was getting into. It was also the first Memorial weekend he didn't know what Randy was doing, and the first three-day holiday he had no plans for Monday afternoon.

He woke up at his usual time the next morning, five-thirty, more tired than when he went to bed. The diner would be busy through lunchtime, he knew, but by mid-afternoon Route A would be bumper-to-bumper with outgoing traffic and he would be free to go somewhere, anywhere, away from the restaurant. He'd go to the May house: might as well make one more visit before that was gone, too.

Will kept to himself most of the morning, avoiding even Winston. But when it was time for the cook to leave, Will ran after him, catching him just as he reached his pickup.

Winston listened to the boy's proposal, his brown eyes shining a little, then said, "I'm glad to give you a ride over there, Will, but you know I'm not crawling around any spook house."

"You just have to stand in it, Win, and help me if I need a taller person. Besides, it's not really spooked."

"It's not spooks that frighten me. It's my knees and ankles, and rotten floorboards. I'm just too old to go adventuring. We've talked about this before— why don't you let me get old, boy?"

"I will, when you are."

"I am, now," said the cook, opening the door of his mud-splattered truck. "Besides, you know I got to get home. Got late seed to put in, more berries to pick, a loft to clean out."

"I thought your sons were back from college."

"They are, and they're working. We all are. Next year's tuition bills are waiting on this year's corn." Winston ran a black, veined hand over the boy's

23

cheek. He was the only person Will still allowed to touch him that way. "You know, Willie, you need a good friend your own age. You need someone you can tell your secrets to without making him worry to death, someone who can listen to your plans without wondering if he should stop you. Understand what I'm saying, boy?"

Will shrugged.

"So how about Ray?"

"He lives on the mainland. They all do."

"A bridge away."

Will didn't reply.

"So—how about—?" The cook nodded in the direction of the grocery. "Couldn't you give him a chance?"

"I guess you are old, Winston."

"That's what I been telling you." He shook his keys. "I'll give you a ride. . . ."

"Thanks," Will replied, his voice flat. "I can get there myself."

He pedaled furiously down Route A, weaving in and out of the packed station wagons and loud carloads of teenagers. His hot tires sang over the grates of the drawbridge, then, on the mainland side of Paradise, grew raspy with sand. Riding on the shoulder of a two-lane road, he headed south along the coast, passing the marina and the commercial harbor, always keeping his eyes on the road, trying not to think about Digger.

About a half mile beyond the harbor, the pavement broke off, West Road becoming two ruts of shell and dust that ran another half mile down to the May Estate. To the left, Will's view of the water was blocked by a widening margin of bay marshes. Pine and deeper wood grew up on the right.

Will could see the house's cupola now, a square of windows rising from the flat roof, above the chimneys, above the trees. Riding past the house, he hid his bike in some bushes and started through the pines that surrounded the building. Underfoot, the needles lay several inches thick, softer than a pile carpet. The air was salty-sweet, a mix of sea and fir smells. Will took deep breaths of it.

At the edge of the clearing he stopped to study the house. Against a growing bank of clouds it looked flat, reminding him of the old photographs he had seen in his history class: black-and-white prints of the May Estate and other summer homes built in the 1920s, and later pictures of the same houses collapsed. In 1929 a hurricane had ripped into the Atlantic coast, and when it finally stopped blowing, East Paradise was a barrier island rather than a township on a small peninsula, and the fine houses across the bay were driftwood. All but the May house.

The weatherboard home had withstood the storm, perhaps because it was larger and better built, said Will's teacher, or because it was further from the water and protected by a small wood. Perhaps. But Will and his friends, and most old shore people, liked to believe it was something unseen that had barred its windows and doors so well, protecting the three-story house from the time it was abandoned, one full year before the storm.

And perhaps that same unseen force had blown up the June storm just ten years ago, the summer Ernest May's oldest grandchild hired a contractor to restore the home. The structure had been reinforced and the rotting center stair torn out when Cordelia blew through. Boarded against the hurricane, the house was not reopened again—at least, not by its original owners.

Sketches of the estate filled Will's history notebook, some of the drawings peopled. He liked to imagine living in a place bigger than six house trailers, a place where a person could get away by simply climbing a stair. He knew that if he ever got rich enough to buy a house, it would have three stories. His parents would be allowed to visit the first floor, his friends to come up to the second. He'd live in the attic.

Having circled the structure once, Will stepped up on the west porch, careful to avoid rotting planks, and proceeded to the back center window. Worked loose by other young people, this entrance to the house had long been in the trust of local kids, who always left the inside shutters closed, the sash pulled down, and the outer shutters wedged together. They knew the sea air would make the wood stick just enough to discourage "outsiders."

Today the window moved more freely than usual. Will stepped back to think a minute. Was somebody already inside? Last fall he and Randy had walked in on four older teenagers passing around a pipe. It was not a scene Will wanted to face alone.

Glancing down he noted that, except for his own faint tracks and some markings made by a fallen pine branch, the porch's sandy surface was smooth. Confident once again, he climbed through the window and, with sudden inspiration, reached back for the tree branch, sweeping his footprints clean.

He drew closed the shutters.

All at once the house enveloped him, dark, airless. Will flicked on his pocket flashlight, shining it around the shelf-lined walls of the room he called the library. Then he tiptoed into the center hall. No need to be quiet, he reasoned; still, he moved silently.

The black-and-white pattern of the tile floor,

bright under his light, receded into darkness. At the far end of the hall he could see a crack of daylight outlining the front door. As he walked toward it he played his beam over the walls, then onto the ceiling. It snagged on four unbroken prisms, the remains of a chandelier that had been somebody's target practice.

Illuminated by only one flashlight, the house seemed larger, darker, and the hole in the center of it, vast. With a dim beam Will traced the wallpaper cutout of the missing steps, whose silhouette rose, turned, and rose again.

The distance between the first and second floors looked to be three times greater than that of other houses Will had visited. Hoping to discover a useable back stair, he and his friends had attempted to pick the locks on the first-floor doors. Unsuccessful, they had knocked on each one, figuring that the most hollow-sounding door would be the best candidate for battering down. But the heavy wooden planking made it almost impossible to hear differences, especially with the giggling and talking that echoed from room to room.

Maybe, being alone, it was time he try again. He thought about the house's layout: three rooms across the back, which he had designated kitchen, library, and billiard room—as in the game of Clue—and two larger, longer rooms on either side of the center hall, which he called the living and dining rooms. Today he'd start in the kitchen, the most likely place to find a service stair.

As he headed toward it Will suddenly pulled up short. Strips of faded, figured paper hung from one wall of the dining room and lay on the floor like a pile of giant confetti. He kicked through the shredded wallpaper: nothing but paste-dried stuff. Moving closer to the ravaged wall he noticed a vertical seam in the plaster.

With his eyes he followed the straight-edged crack to another one that ran horizontally. Suddenly he realized that the lines were part of a box shape recessed into the wall. Within this area, bare spots gleamed like painted wood. Will touched the surface, then knocked sharply. Hollow!

Pulling aside a fringe of paper strips, he found an indentation in the wood and, above that, a bolt. He grasped the metal rod. "Please slide."

It did, but the warped panel would not budge. Will flicked off his dimming flashlight. Setting it on the floor, he tried again, one hand in the finger niche, the other flat against the wood.

Suddenly the panel slid to the right, banging hard against the inner wall. The entire house echoed with the noise.

Will judged the opening to be about three-and-a-half feet wide, not quite as high or deep. Unable to take his eyes off the gaping wall, he groped for his flashlight but lost it in the heap of wallpaper. Just then he heard something.

Footsteps. The echoing house made it difficult to determine their direction. They seemed to be getting louder, then stopped, proceeding more softly. Was the person headed away from him? Will wondered. Or, aware of another's presence, was the walker trying to move quietly?

Should he call out? Or should he hide?

Waving his hand around the inside of the closet, hoping that it was indeed empty, Will climbed in and eased the door shut.

4
Footsteps and Toes

WITH THE PANEL CLOSED, SOUND WAS MUFFLED inside the wall. Still, Will sensed the approach of someone and goosebumped all over. There had been only one set of footsteps, and none of Will's friends ever came to the house alone. I must have been crazy to, he thought.

Now Will could hear the floor outside the cupboard creaking beneath the person's weight. He held his breath.

"Hello?" the walker called.

Sam! His neighbor Sam! The kid had come here by himself and figured out how to get in. Clever guy.

Furious for getting worked up over Wax Lips, Will was ready to burst out of the cupboard. Then he had a better idea: Moving his face close to the crack, he mewed softly. A minute passed in silence. Will whined again. Very, very lightly he scratched a nail against the wood panel.

Will heard Sam take a step forward. He knew the boy was close and gave another low half-mew. The cupboard's bolt flicked one way, then the other. The door cracked and a hairline of yellow light shone in. The beam disappeared for a long minute, then danced back up the wall into the cupboard.

As the door began to slide back, Will pushed it from his side, then bounced up from his knees with a loud shriek.

Bam! The panel slid back, shaking the cupboard floor with its force. The boy didn't tiptoe now. Will heard Sam's feet pounding hard and fast—out of the room, down the center hall—and doubled over, trying to hold in the laughter till he was sure he was alone again. He wished he could have gotten a better look at the boy's face. His pale hair was probably standing on end. It would be great to be at the grocery and hear the story Sam would tell.

When the house had settled back into its musty quiet, Will, still chuckling to himself, placed his hands against the door to slide it open. The panel would not move. He exerted greater pressure. The door felt as if it were pinned closed.

Now Will's mind reeled backwards as he tried to recall what he had heard when the thing slammed shut. Had there been a click? Had Sam bolted in the wild animal?

And now he's off to the grocery, Will thought, to tell a story too fantastic for anyone to believe. And I'm left here until someone smells me out, probably Al. Will could imagine how his classmate would brag about finding the only real corpse in the spook house. Oh yes, Will said to himself, this cupboard will make a fine coffin.

He sprang into action. "Sam!" he shouted, banging his hands, kicking his feet against the wall. "It's me, Will. Come back, Sam, please come back!" he called over and over. Worn out and discouraged, he slumped against the cupboard wall.

The floor in the dining room creaked. Just the house's old bones, Will said to himself, cracking and settling.

Maybe. Or maybe someone was in the house, close by, standing on a loose board.

What if the kid wasn't pedaling frantically across the bridge? Will thought. What if, feeling secure, even proud of himself for locking the beast in the closet, Sam had turned back, curious? What if, at that very moment, he was standing on the other side of the sliding door, snickering?

In as cool a voice as Will could muster, he said, "I know you're there, Sam."

Silence.

Will wondered how long it took to suffocate. He became more and more aware of a peculiar smell. How would he look partially decayed? Would anyone recognize him?

"Sam," he called out, "are you there?"

He thought he heard a noise and continued with fresh hope. "What is it you want from me, Sam, twenty-five bucks? You got it, all of it. Berries paid in full."

No response.

"Maybe you want another apology. Is that it? You want me to say I'm sorry? I'm sorry."

Still not a sound.

"Look, I scared you. You scared me. We're even. Now let me out."

Silence.

"Okay, not quite even. I called you some names. And I could have been a little wrong when—" Will broke off. This was turning into a lousy confession.

Still, the cupboard was growing warmer, stinkier by the minute.

"Please, Sam."

What would his buddies think if they saw him now, entertaining Wax Lips? Funny thing, Will reflected, the kid had appeared to be a soft touch. Perhaps it was dangerous to push sensitive types too far. They probably didn't get over things easily.

Will cast about for another strategy. If he caught the kid off guard with a desperate appeal—"Snake! Snake! There's a snake in here. Help!"

The bolt snapped back, the door slid open.

Will couldn't resist. "Fooled you!" he crowed.

"Quiet!" said Sam. "Somebody's coming."

At first, Will didn't believe him and tried to squirm out while the boy climbed in. Then he heard the shutters slam against the wall at the back of the house. Groaning, he pulled his legs back in and, with Sam's help, slid the cupboard door shut once more.

Side by side Will and Sam crouched, filling up the width of the compartment.

"What's in here?" asked Sam.

"Besides us?"

"Something smells. Smells bad. If we had a little more space, I could reach my flashlight." The boy pressed against Will, trying to work his arm around to his left pocket. "Yours is in my right back pocket," he told Will. "Can you get it?"

"*My* flashlight?" Will choked.

"You left it in the rubble on the floor," Sam said. "Can we stand up in here?" He raised his hands to feel above them. "If we stood, we'd both be a lot skinnier."

"You knew! You knew the whole time!" Will almost shouted. "When you ran out of here, you were faking."

"Shhh! We got company." Sam lowered his arms. "We're stuck. There's a ceiling about a foot above us."

Will did not reply. He could feel his neighbor's shoulders begin to shake and knew that Wax Lips wasn't trembling with fear.

Sam snorted into his hand. "Sorry," he whispered. "It was funny."

"Real funny."

Sam's body tensed, grew still, then the boy began to hiccup. Will ground his teeth. To be laughed at was miserable enough; to be laughed at by someone acting polite . . . "Go ahead. Get hysterical," said Will.

"It was funny," Sam repeated, his hiccups finally subsiding. After several minutes he asked, "Are your legs hurting?"

"Roll forward on your knees."

He followed Will's example. "I haven't heard any more footsteps. Think we can get out of this box?"

Just as Sam spoke, thumping, wooden sounds came from the room behind them.

"Somebody's in the kitchen," Will whispered, "searching cupboards."

Suddenly the wall behind them banged. Both boys jumped, then stared straight ahead at their shadows, sharp against the illuminated panel. Their back ends felt cooler.

"This is a pretty sight," said Toes, shining her flashlight at them. "Two rump roasts in the pantry closet."

Will and Sam turned to look at her at the same time and knocked heads.

She raised an eyebrow.

"You finished the freezer cases awfully quick," Sam said to his sister as Will backed out of the compartment into the kitchen.

"I made a deal with Mom and Dad," Toes replied. "Knew you were up to something, little brother, but didn't think I'd find you hanging around with *him*."

Sam glanced at Will and swung his feet over the side of the two-way cupboard. Then, stretching across it, he slid open the front panel. A draft swept between the rooms.

"A dumbwaiter!" exclaimed Toes, peering through the gap. "That must be the dining room."

"It is," replied Sam, "but this is just a cupboard. It doesn't have ropes, or holes for ropes. Besides, there's a ceiling."

"It's a dumbwaiter," she insisted, shining the light around the inside of the compartment, then turning it on Will. He was standing several feet back from the opening, staring at it in amazement. "What are you thinking?" she demanded.

"This opening wasn't here before," he said. "At least, it wasn't visible."

"No?" Her eyes were bright. "What was?"

"A wall of shelves," Will answered. "Narrow shelves, the kind you stack dishes on."

"Guess this is what's left of them," Sam said, running the beam of his flashlight up and down a pile of planks. He dragged one over to measure it against the opening. "What do you know about the wallpaper?" he asked. "The scraping looks new to me."

"The paper was one piece in April," Will replied, following the boy into the next room.

Toes crawled through the opening. "Somebody's after something," she asserted. "I wonder what they were hoping to find in here?"

"I wonder why that cupboard was covered to begin with." Sam turned to Will. "Do you know anything about the people who lived here?"

He thought a moment. "The builder's sons fought a lot, and there's something about a funny will. My mother would know the story, or Ms. Kilborn, my teacher— No, she's been living here awhile but she's not real shore people."

"How long does it take to become real shore people?"

Toes rolled her eyes at Sam's question, then propelled herself from the wall into the room. "Someone must have been hiding valuables," she theorized. "Or something illegal!"

"Well, anything they were hiding is gone now," said Will.

Sam shone his light around the two-way compartment, running his hand over its inner surface. "You know, you may be right, Toes. These floor boards could have been nailed down on top of the tray. And look, the grain of the ceiling is different from the walls. Maybe it was put in later. If this is a dumbwaiter"—his voice grew more excited—"and we can rip loose a few boards, we could get upstairs."

Will walked over to the opening.

"All we'd have to do is get a ladder or nail some blocks to the wall for toeholds, and once we're up the chute, we can hang a rope"—Sam glanced at Will—"unless you know an easier way."

"I don't."

"So when are you free next?"

Toes scowled.

39

Will ignored her. "Tomorrow afternoon?"

"Stock day," said Sam. "Thursday morning?"

"I still have school."

After agreeing on three o'clock Friday afternoon, the boys followed Toes into the main hall. Sam stopped to look in the living room. The spacious room was the only one on the first floor with curtains, one long drape hanging from a side window, another piled at its base.

"Have you ever moved before?" Sam's voice slapped against the walls.

"No."

"This is how it sounds," he told Will. "Hollowlike. Too big. They take out all your furniture and sit it on the front street. Everyone stares at it. And you walk around inside, feeling like you're lost in your own house."

"Do you want to go back to—"

"My parents say we won't."

Toes came to the doorway and gazed silently at her brother for a few moments. "Come on, Sam," she said at last. "You know Mom needs help this time of day."

5

A Little Show Business

FIVE-THIRTY TUESDAY EVENING, AS WILL WAS backing through the diner's swinging doors, he noticed Toes sitting at the counter.

"When you get a minute," she called.

"Right." He gritted his teeth, dumped the dishes he was carrying by the washer's big rubber flaps, then offered to help one of the waitresses with a large order.

"Why you sweet thing!" she exclaimed.

After assisting her with a second order, he poured coffee, chatting with each of the customers.

"I've known this young man since he was pushing a corn popper round the diner," an old volunteer fireman told younger conventioneers.

Will fetched a dozen packets of catsup for a teen-ager, apologized to an elderly couple for spotted silverware, helped lift a child into a booster seat, and managed to smile when the kid threw spaghetti at him.

Toes, to Will's surprise, didn't look a bit put off by her long wait. He decided to try one more task. As he strode past his mother and Winston, however, Mrs. Hanson caught him by an apron string.

"What?" he grunted.

"Yes, Mother?" she prompted.

"Yes, Mother?" He almost whispered.

"Isn't that the girl next door?" Mrs. Hanson nod-ded toward Toes.

"Yes'm."

"Is she here to see you, or is she waiting to be served? She has been very patient."

"I . . . uh . . . I'll find out."

He headed toward the counter but was inter-cepted by a customer. During the man's drawn-out story Will overheard Winston talking to his mother. "You know I don't like to interfere, Barbara," the cook said, "but knowing my own sons, I can't help but think it'd be better if you grabbed Willie by the sleeve."

Out of the corner of his eye Will saw the puzzled

look on his mother's face. "His father has never objected—"

"I know. We're talking about Will. And just this summer. Maybe by next year. . ."

Will moved on, finishing the sentence in his head: The boy will grow out of it.

He had spent his whole life growing out of it in front of the cooks, waitresses, food suppliers, members of the city council, and annual conventioneers.

"What do you want?" he growled at Toes.

"A twenty-foot ladder." She turned her stool to face him. "If we nail blocks to the wall, anyone will be able to climb to the second floor."

Will could feel his mother and Winston watching him. "I'll be back."

Whizzing through the kitchen he scooped up a plate of french fries, then, reentering the dining area, punched the button on the soda machine and sent the plate and glass skidding toward the girl, followed by a salt shaker. Onto the counter he tossed packets of catsup.

"This is nice, but I said I wanted a ladder."

They both stared at the food.

"Do you have any mustard?"

Sighing, Will bent down and scrounged beneath the counter.

"I've been pricing them," she began, "and it's

going to take a lot of overtime at the grocery, a lot of tips from you. Do you know where we can borrow one?"

Will straightened up, thinking. Was this the kind of thing to ask Winston? "Maybe . . . "

"He's training them," Toes sneered.

"What?"

"I've been watching the people in this place. What a show!"

Will glanced around. "Yeah."

"The man right there is training the new waitresses. I bet he does it every year."

Will followed her eyes to Mr. Dan, who was talking and joking with the staff.

"He teaches them what he likes, just how he likes it, rewarding them for a cheap meal with a big tip"— she lowered the Coke in her glass a full inch and a half with one breath—"so that they fuss over him whenever he comes, making him feel important. Am I right?"

Will watched Mr. Dan for a moment.

"I am," she said confidently. "So where are we going to get a ladder?"

"I have to think about it."

Toes gurgled the soda at the bottom of her glass, then held out her hand. "Check."

Will blinked, surprised that she would offer to pay for what she hadn't ordered.

"Your mother is working the cash register now. Won't she wonder if I just walk past?" The girl leaned forward. "I mean, that was the whole point, wasn't it? You served me so it didn't look like I came visiting. You don't expect me to believe you were acting neighborly?"

"No, I don't," Will answered, pulling out a pad and pencil.

"Must I tip?"

Will scowled.

Toes sat back, turning slowly on her stool, panning the diner. She stopped suddenly and Will glanced in the same direction as she.

"Who's that?"

"Olivia Winters," Will replied, nodding respectfully to the lady approaching them.

Toes stared. "How old is she?"

"Sixty-something."

The slender woman, dressed in jeans and a button-down shirt, had the walk of a teenage boy. She wore no makeup. Her hair, a mix of yellow and gray, shone like rope fiber, parted and curled in an old-fashioned hairstyle that fit her head like a cap.

"Miss Olivia," Will greeted her. "You never come round summer season."

"Now that the business is out of my hands, I've time I didn't used to," the woman replied, glancing at Mr. Dan, who quickly became engrossed in his dessert. "Too much time. That's why I'm here nosing in other people's business."

Will smiled. "We're always glad to see you."

"That's what your papa said. I brought you—" She stopped and returned Toes' stare. "Am I interrupting something?"

"No," Will said quickly. "No," he repeated, tearing off Toes' bill, slapping it on the counter, and flicking his head to the right.

The girl made no effort to move on.

"I found something," the woman continued, opening her hand. "Thought you might want it, boy."

Will looked down at the dull metal tag.

"I'm real sorry about your dog."

Will said nothing.

"Found this in my yard," she told him, placing the engraved disk in his hand. "You know how Digger and Old Gold liked to play."

Will nodded wordlessly.

"I loved to watch them play. You could hardly tell one from the other." Miss Olivia's voice dropped.

Will closed his hand over the tag, squeezing it until its metal edge cut into his palm. "Can—can I get you something to eat?" he asked.

"No. I don't have much appetite anymore. And they don't like people smoking over coffee anywhere these days." Her green eyes searched Will's face. "You know, Old Gold is a father again, by a pretty little bitch. I got pick of the litter."

"Good," Will replied without enthusiasm.

"He'll be weaned in a few weeks."

"Are you sure I can't get you some coffee?" Will asked.

"I'd like to give you the pup."

"No."

"Maybe you want to talk it over with your mama."

"No," Will said, his mouth tight.

Keeping her eyes on him, Miss Olivia withdrew a cigarette from a silver case. "You and I are a lot alike," she said. "We just don't want to let go. But you got to, boy. They take it from you anyway, the past, the present. You got to let go, keep going— or so they tell me."

She glanced over at Mr. Dan, who had no more bread pudding to push around. "Daniel," she said with a sharp nod, then turned and left.

Retreating to the kitchen, Will walked circles around the stoves. When he reentered the dining area, Toes, who was still sitting at the counter, glanced up from a menu as if she wanted to say something.

"What?" he snarled.

"You didn't write anything on the check." The softness of Toes' voice surprised him.

47

Will scribbled "Fries," scratched it out, wrote "Soda," and handed her the tab with some of his tip money, enough to cover one large Coke.

She looked at him, tilting her head to one side, shaking it. "You must be the first guy in history to buy a girl a drink just to prove you can't stand her."

6

To the Top

WHEN WILL TURNED ONTO WEST ROAD FRIDAY
afternoon he found the MacDowells waiting for him,
bulging knapsacks strapped to the rear of their bikes,
Schaefer sitting on a towel in Toes' front basket.

Sam greeted Will with a big smile. Toes wel-
comed him with "We were here at three, like you
said."

Will eyed the dog.

"So where are we going?" Toes asked, sitting lop-
sided on her bike seat, kicking up dust with one
foot.

"To the harbor. To get pieces of a ladder."

Toes pedaled off as if she divined Will's plan. He
wished that she did so he could wait for her and

49

Sam at the May house. He rode with the MacDowells in silence, turning at the last possible moment onto Horseshoe Road, which curved along the border of the commercial harbor. Pumping hard toward the dockside market, he tried not to think about Digger.

But Will couldn't help but think about his old dog. Between the tiny weatherboard houses and mobile homes were yards of tall grass strewn with rotting nets and lobster traps, splintered planks and red floats and dock bumpers and nylon cord and broken shells and decaying crabs—once playgrounds for Digger and him—for a long time, the edge of Will's world.

"Here," he shouted over his shoulder, jumping off his bike at the fish market, walking it across the front of the long building. At the boundary of the lot he had planned to raid he stopped short.

Sam bumped into him. "Something wrong?"

"That trailer wasn't here before," Will said thoughtfully, then shrugged and pointed out several topless wooden boxes, explaining how they could be stacked on their sides to create a ladder.

"We're allowed to take these?" Sam asked.

Will followed the boy's gaze to the slatted blinds of the unfamiliar trailer.

"Just act like we can. Act like we've got permission, and anyone watching will think we do."

50

"Maybe you better wait for us on the road, Sam," Toes said.

"No, these things are heavy," Will told her. "Everybody's got to carry."

"But he can't act."

"What?"

Sam blushed.

"He can't pretend. If Sam thinks someone thinks he's guilty, he looks it even if he's not."

"That's the dumbest thing I ever heard," said Will.

Sam's color deepened. He laid his bike down in the grass and strode toward the pile of boxes.

At that moment a young man with curly blond hair emerged from the trailer. He glanced at Toes and Will, then Sam, who continued toward the crates without hesitation. Nodding pleasantly to the three of them, the stranger went on down the road.

"Maybe you don't know your brother as well as you think," Will remarked.

"I know him better than you do."

The trailer door opened again.

Sam, with his arms around a box, looked up at the squarely built man, then back at Will and Toes.

"Willie, Willie Hanson! Good to see you over here," the man greeted him. "I thought you had forgotten about my side of the bay."

"Hello, Mr. Wyeth."

51

"Things humming at the diner? Mom and Dad looked busy last weekend."

"The usual for this time of year."

"So what brings you and . . . and . . ." He looked at Will's companions.

"Sam," the blushing boy introduced himself, putting down the crate and offering his hand. "Sam MacDowell. I live next door to Will."

"Pleased to meet you, Sam MacDowell. And you?"

Toes looked Mr. Wyeth up and down.

"What's your name, missy?"

"Toes."

He repeated her name. "That's no ordinary-mary. Any reason why they call you that?"

"Yes."

Henry Wyeth waited.

Toes gazed at him steadily, but said nothing.

"You kin to pink Sam here?"

"Yes."

"My older sister," the boy said, brushing his cheek with the palm of his hand.

Mr. Wyeth nodded. "How old are you, Miss Toes?"

"Thirteen. How old are you?"

"Forty-four," the fleet owner replied, then broke out laughing and winked at Sam and Will. "You boys got your hands full."

Toes' eyes narrowed.

Sam looked at his sister until she returned his gaze, then he said, "Mr. Wyeth, we could really use a box or two. Do you think we could borrow them for the afternoon?"

"A box or two, I don't see why not."

"Or six," Will said quickly.

"Six, now. You sure you all don't need more. . . ."

"We'll return them," Sam assured the man.

"No need. No need. Help yourself, boys and girl," he added, glancing one more time at Toes before he moved on toward the market.

Sweating, breathless, they stood in the cupola, Will looking east, Toes west, Sam turning round and round, as if he were trying to gather all 360 degrees of land, sea, and sky in one eyeful.

We did it! Will wanted to shout. We did it!

Sam bumped into him, then sat hard on one of the window benches. "We did it," he said proudly.

"Yes." Toes dropped down on the window seat adjacent to her brother, rubbing her rope-sore hands.

Though the three of them had argued most of the way, they had pulled together when necessary, lowering the ceiling in one piece, stacking boxes inside the chute. Toes clawed her way through cobwebs and dropped two dead mice on the boys. From the wall opening on the second floor, she hung a rope ladder for Sam and Will to climb.

On the upper floor they discovered an old iron tub full of trash, some straight-back chairs, and, in the room above the kitchen, a partially opened door. A set of steps ran down to the first floor—ending behind the locked kitchen door, Will guessed—and up to the third. A small spiral stair took them from the third floor to the cupola.

Feeling tired but pleased with their accomplishment, Will took a seat across from Toes. Schaefer, who had journeyed by knapsack, leaped onto the bench next to him.

"He likes you," Sam observed.

"Schaefer likes the way he smells," Toes corrected her brother. "When you sweat," she told Will, "you smell like diner food. It must be cooked into your clothes."

Will frowned at her, then turned his cheek against the window glass. Out of the corner of his eye he saw Sam shake his head in disagreement.

"I don't think that's it," the boy said. "It's not just the smell."

Will fought the urge to stick his nose in his shirt.

Swinging her feet up on the bench, Toes gestured at the blue that swept each side of the long, shining island. "You know, I can almost see it. From a distance you might think it's paradise." When Will looked surprised, she added quickly, "If you really use your imagination."

Pushing the dog aside, Will rose silently and descended the spiral stair. Randy would have liked it here, he thought; he would have taken rolls of pictures from the cupola and from the shutterless third floor, whose low-ceilinged rooms floated in dusty light. Will tried out the various pieces of straw and oak furniture, posing one way, then another, as Randy would have asked him to.

Ten minutes later Sam and Toes joined him, and the three took the back stairway all the way down to the first floor. Will tinkered with the inside latch; Sam whooped as they emerged into the kitchen.

After the wash of sunlight at the top of the house, the first floor seemed darker than ever. They walked slowly.

At first Will thought he was imagining what he saw. Then he felt Sam and Toes grow still next to him. Curls of wallpaper picked up, floated, dropped down to the floor.

"A draft." Toes' voice broke the silence.

"From where?" asked Sam.

Toes suddenly picked up her leg: A long twist of paper encircled her ankle.

"The back of the house," Will said.

They hurried toward the library. Just as they entered the window shutter banged back. All three jumped.

"I thought we closed this." Sam stuck his head out the window and looked left and right.

"The house is haunted," Toes replied.

"Could be," said Sam.

Will turned to him. Now that was a great idea!

7

Suspicions

"HAUNT IT?" SAM REPEATED.

"And charge admission," said Toes. "Cut it three ways, do a series of tours!"

Will nodded, surprised by Toes' show of enthusiasm.

Pedaling back to the mainland that day, and during work breaks Saturday and Sunday, the kids talked about the kind of spook house they wanted to create. Sam suggested writing a story about the Mays, entwined with crimes and tragedies, making the tour an eerie family history.

While discussing possible scenes, they negotiated roles: Will begged to be tour guide; Toes chose for herself dramatic cameo appearances; Sam accepted behind-the-scenes work.

Preparation tasks were divided equally. Sam volunteered to take inventory of the house and to shop the boardwalk for items such as cheap, smashable glassware, a rubber mask, and a large picture of a person's face—somebody dignified—"not Jesus, and not Michael Jackson," Toes instructed.

Her job was to draft accurate floor plans for blocking out the tour. She also volunteered to do the audio work, taping organ music and recording rifle shots and screams at the amusement pier. Will, assigned house security, was to nail down the "community window" and free up another, as well as work on the back door so it could be opened from the inside. His off-site chore was, as Sam dubbed it, "food tech."

The following Tuesday, just before the diner's evening crew took over the stoves, Will boiled up a large pot of spaghetti and carried it out to the loading dock. He was busy dishing pasta into containers of varying food color when he noticed Winston's flour-dusted shoes standing next to him. The cook squatted by Will, picking up one by one the bowls of bloodred, deep purple, and slimy green-yellow noodles. "Yuck."

I don't have to explain, Will thought; "yuck" is not a question.

Winston looked at Will expectantly, then took a more comfortable position on the top step and lit a cigarette.

"Had to open another case of catsup yesterday," the cook began. "Just opened one last week. What do you make of that?"

"People prefer catsup to mustard?" Will proposed half-heartedly. He knew that he had never been good at lying to Winston.

"Oh, I think people like it just as much as they always did. No more, no less."

Will shrugged.

"Went to make lasagna for yesterday's special. Now I know, I *know* I had three tins of tomato sauce in that pantry."

Will looked away.

"I got just two questions for you, boy, and I want an honest answer to each."

Will picked up the gory red spaghetti and twisted it in his hands. The cook eyed it and took another puff on his cigarette.

"First off, are you doing with your head on straight?"

"Trust me, Winston."

"I'm trying. I'm trying." He held up two fingers. "Second, are there any other supplies that are going to suddenly disappear on me?"

"Eggs, but just a few, in about two weeks.

And . . . uh . . . about the same time," Will ventured, "we sure could use some liver."

" 'We,' " the cook repeated to himself. Snuffing out his cigarette, he stood up. "Use your head," he said as he turned back toward the kitchen. "I don't want to find you kids in trouble, understand? I don't want to find you hurt."

Will nodded.

"I'll see what I can do about the liver."

Three days later Will pedaled from school to the May house in high spirits. He had survived a year with Ms. Kilborn and bore written proof in his back pocket.

He, Sam, and Toes worked hard that afternoon and, on their return from the house, stopped to wash up at a gas station at the head of Horseshoe Road. Will was coming out of the men's room, toweling the last bit of black paint off his hands, when he ran into Jenko.

As Will and his school chum talked, Sam turned away to fill his bike tire with air. But Toes—even as she put her money in the Coke machine, punched the button, pulled the ring off the can, and lifted it to her mouth—kept her eyes on Will.

She's reading my lips, Will thought, waiting for me to blab about the house.

It wasn't long before Jenko noticed Toes' watchful
eyes. Will knew that because of the way his buddy
spread his legs, flexed them (little wisps of hair
caught the wind), and thrust out his chest while
telling Will his unhappy tale: Having lured pink-
nailed Sheila to the house, Jenko discovered the
window nailed shut—and the mosquitos were bad
that night.

Will could hardly keep from laughing and Jenko,
basking in Toes' attentiveness, began to smile. He
strutted a little and talked louder. Will kept his own
voice deliberately soft.

Then Toes, realizing that Jenko's performance was
for her, took a step back, torn between her instinct
to flee and her desire to make certain that Will kept
their pact. Will leaned close to Jenko, as if he were
giving away secrets, and would have continued the
act another ten minutes if fire sirens hadn't sounded
nearby.

Sam threw down the air hose. Toes scooped up
Schaefer, dropped him in her basket. Jenko hopped
on Will's bike before he did. "I can pedal for two
of us," he shouted, pulling Will on by his waist. Will
had no choice but to ride the bar.

They chased the engines and a police car down
to the fish market. They dropped their bikes in
the grass and ran toward the wharf, Toes leading

the way, Jenko close behind. Will stopped to pick up Schaefer, who was bunny-hopping toward the commotion.

Fifteen-foot flames shot upward from nets spooled at the back of a steel fishing boat. A fireboat moved into position. Men on shore continually doused the dock so the flames would not spread to land.

A crowd gathered and two policemen worked to keep them back from the dock. Will saw Mr. Wyeth standing apart from the rest, his arms crossed, his face expressionless. Several feet beyond him stood Miss Olivia, her face as still as Mr. Wyeth's as she gazed at the burning nets of the boat she once owned.

The blaze was extinguished without incident and the bystanders began to speculate on the fire's cause. Will watched Mr. Wyeth talk with the police sergeant, who continually shook his head in disagreement.

"You're foolish not to investigate, Henry," he heard the policeman say. "Your captain claims those nets were too damp to burn by themselves. Somebody primed them."

Mr. Wyeth studied his boat for several moments, then answered, "But it's my choice, isn't it, whether to request an investigation or simply report the incident?"

"There's the matter of insurance—"

"I'm running a business, Stu. The nets are replaceable within a day. Investigations run weeks. As for insurance, nets are affordable, Mutual's rate hikes are not."

"You know this could happen again."

"Could," replied Mr. Wyeth, surveying the crowd around him, his eyes pausing at Miss Olivia. "Could." He turned abruptly to face the sergeant.

"It's no secret that there are people around here who are not fond of me, fishing people reluctant to see the family-owned business a thing of the past. These people may feel they have cause to . . . play pranks. And you could prove that they did, but I would not press charges. You'll have to pardon me, Stu, but this is a fishermen's affair, and we fishing people, despite our quarrels, feel a certain loyalty to our kind."

"It's your choice, Henry. I just hope you're not asking for more trouble."

Will noticed a few fishermen eyeing Miss Olivia, and found himself doing the same. She met their looks steadily, without warmth, until she turned to Will.

Her face softened then, just a little, but that small change in expression made him feel guilty for wondering if she would set a fire.

"You remember my offer, boy," she said, glancing at him, then Schaefer, who was still in Will's arms. "Think again."

Henry Wyeth looked over at Will, as if the boy had disrupted his thoughts.

Putting her fingers to her lips, Miss Olivia whistled sharply. Old Gold bounded out from behind some bass traps, so much like Digger the sight took away Will's breath. He watched the two of them go down the road until the dog was no longer in sight.

8
Trouble

WILL WAS SUPPOSED TO BE AT THE POST OFFICE, one block east of where he was standing now, at Riply's Marina and Boatyard, "Rip-off's," as the locals called it.

The invitations were in his knapsack, white cards inscribed with fluid black letters:

MacHan, Inc.
presents
Sunset Tours
for those not easily frightened . . .

Sunday, June 18, 7 PM   *Regrets only*
The May House   *Will, the Diner*

Will carried the envelopes, too, and at that moment was supposed to be buying stamps at the post office, sending the invitations out in Wednesday's four o'clock mail.

A waste of time, he thought as he walked up and down the slips, looking at the secondhand boats. Twice he had told Sam that he was meeting his buddies on the boardwalk that night and could hand-deliver the invitations.

But no, Sam said, Toes didn't want that. Jenko and Al might ask a lot of questions.

"And you think I'm going to spill the beans!" Will challenged. Sam had looked away, embarrassed.

Now Will glanced at his watch: ten minutes to four. Maybe he'd mail the invitations, maybe he wouldn't. First, he'd check out the power boats.

He was headed toward the motor craft when he pulled up short. Of all times for Mr. MacDowell to be out browsing! What if Sam and Toes learned that Will was here instead of at the post office?

But Mr. MacDowell hadn't noticed him yet. The man talked seriously with Mr. Riply and pointed to a Sunfish. Will also looked at the little boat: It had known better days.

Now Mr. Riply nodded at Mr. MacDowell and smiled a little. Or maybe his mouth naturally bowed up—like a fox's, Will thought.

Mr. MacDowell took out his checkbook. At that moment Nate Riply looked up and nodded at Will, little bits of his teeth showing. Will saw Sam's father accept Mr. Riply's pen. He hesitated, then called out, "Hi, Mr. MacDowell."

The marina owner looked surprised.

"Hello, Will." Mr. MacDowell smiled. "Come on over and look at my new boat."

Will took a few steps closer and glanced down at the Sunfish. "Guess you—guess you got a real good deal on this one," he said.

Sam's father stopped writing. "Oh yes? Is Mr. Riply here famous for his good deals?"

Will swallowed hard. "He's good to locals, for sure."

Sam's father glanced from Will to Mr. Riply and back again. Will didn't dare look at the boatyard owner.

"Maybe," said Mr. MacDowell, "this is the kind of thing I should talk over with your father, Will. I believe I've been too hasty. I know I have. I was hoping to surprise Sam and Toes . . . but . . . your father would know a good boat, a good boat for people your age." He closed his checkbook and looked solemnly at Mr. Riply.

The owner shrugged and walked away.

When he was gone Mr. MacDowell turned to

Will. "Thanks, son, I appreciate your advice. Do you know how to handle one of these little Sunfish?"

"I used to sail Randy's."

"Good. I'll feel more easy about it, then, when Sam and Toes are learning."

"It takes time," Will told his neighbor, "a lot of watching, to learn to read the water. But all the sudden, you know how. All the sudden, you know you can."

Mr. MacDowell nodded. "I figured I could rely on you."

Will's night out with his old buddies was a bore. The boardwalk's Haunted Mansion, with its ply-wood windows and two-dimensional bats and grace-less spiderwebs painted on the front—no foul smells, nothing gross to touch, nothing as fine as shattering green goblets, the same shrieks over and over and the four-minute tour from beginning to end made in a wheeled car—was safe and boring.

Will could hardly wait to get home and tell Sam and Toes about the lousy spook house, to predict the triumph of theirs.

But the evening dragged on. He found it difficult to concentrate on Jenko's long stories and missed several punch lines. Neal annoyed him by repeat-edly shoving coins into a claw machine, dropping the prize every time. When, in the video arcade, Al jumped up and down and yelled, "I killed the Scummies! I killed the Scummies!" Will laughed out loud, then noticed that his other friends did not.

Only Ray didn't get on Will's nerves, until he asked for the third time, "What's going on with you?"

He and Will had joined a crowd at the window of the Lifesaving Station, looking at old postcards and pictures of Paradise. Will was studying a rough sketch of the May Estate when he heard someone say in a low voice, "That's the house we were talking about. You can see how it would . . ." Will spun around, knocking Ray back a step.

"Easy, Will. What's . . . ?"

But he looked past his schoolmate, searching the crowd for the speaker.

Two middle-aged men and a woman, a red-eyed teenager and his girl, and a pair of summer police officers looked back at him. Several people departed from the rear of the crowd.

You can see how it would—what? Be a great house to fix up? An easy place to knock down? To hide out? Stash some drugs? Haunt? To catch some kids.

"Will," prompted Ray, "have you heard anything I just said?"

"Sure." Nothing to worry about, he told himself.

Somebody talking to talk. Probably the man with the sunburned arms and blue Hawaiian shirt.

Ray waved his hand in front of Will's face. "What's going on with you?"

It was a relief, two hours later, to shout from the diner's loading dock, "I'm back. Be in in a few minutes."

"Willie—" His mother came to the screen door.

"Ma'am?"

"There's someone waiting for you. Out front."

Will frowned and entered the kitchen. He hadn't wanted it to be this way. Though he had seen the pink come up in Sam's face when he canceled out of that night's rehearsal, he had hoped the boy would understand how much he wanted to be with his old buddies. He had wished Sam would act cool, not waiting like a puppy for Will to return, not pouting like he was the sensitive type who . . .

Will pushed through the swinging doors and found Toes sitting alone at the counter, staring down at a chocolate soda. Her mouth was on the straw; she sucked up nothing.

Will had never seen her with her shoulders hunched and wasn't sure what to do. He walked by her twice, hoping she'd look up and give him some cue. Though he wasn't hungry, he fixed a bowl of rice pudding and a glass of milk and banged them down on the counter next to her. Toes pulled her soda closer.

"So," said Will.

"So," said Toes, "you've given your pals the invites?"

Will drew in his breath, then said in a low, distinct voice, "I mailed them. I mailed them four-thirty today. Sam told me I had to mail them. Because you said I had to mail them. So don't play dumb, Toes!"

"That's your game, Will, not mine." She took a long sip. "As for the invitations, Sam told *me* that we should trust you."

"Well I wish he'd make up his mind."

"Don't criticize him."

"I wasn't criticizing. I was pointing out that—"

"We have a problem," she interrupted.

"You mean, a new one?"

She stirred her soda with a straw, then pushed the glass away. "I hope you feel bad about this," she began.

"Something tells me I will." He came around the counter and sat down next to her.

"Sam and I went to the house to do some work tonight."

"Yeah? Where is he?" Will asked, eager to tell the boy about the boardwalk spook house.

"He's not back yet."

Will glanced at the clock above the kitchen door. "Kind of late to be there alone," he said uneasily.

"He isn't," Toes replied. "He's with my parents. At the ER."

"The emergency room!" Will jumped up.

"Well at least I know you're not a complete jerk."

Will sat down. "Tell me," he said quietly, "in a normal person's way, as best you can, what happened."

The girl passed her hand quickly over her eyes.

"Is he—hurting?"

"I think he hurt—a lot—at first," she said. "His foot. But he's okay. Okay. *Okay*." She made herself rigid. "It's probably just a bad sprain. He said—I yelled louder than him, when I saw him fall. In the house, alone, I didn't know what to do—should I stay with him, should I run for help. He banged his head and I didn't know—

"If I get the hiccups, Will, I'll have them all night."

Will looked around to see if anyone was watching, then nudged the soda toward her. "Drink," he urged gently. "Come on, Toes. A little more."

She did and her body slowly relaxed.

Fifteen minutes later the lights went on over the grocery and Toes jumped up. She started for the door, then turned around, pulling bills out of her pocket, looking at Will expectantly.

He strolled around the counter and picked up the empty dishes. "If you pay," he said, backing through the silver doors, "my mother's going to wonder."

9
Tough Questions

THE NEXT MORNING SAM HOBBLED INTO THE DINER on crutches. A mild sprain, the doctor had told him. The injury would heal if he stayed off the ankle, one week, maybe two. "The tour's in four days. What are we going to do?" the boy asked, sinking down at the end of an empty booth.

"Looks to me as if you get around pretty good," Will encouraged his neighbor. "You made it over here."

"I get around all right, but I can't sneak around." Sam pounded the crutch on the floor. "You know they'll hear me."

"Yeah."

Will flapped menus against his thigh and stared

down at the bandaged foot. He tried to feel as worried and sorry as he had when Toes told him the details of the accident. He tried to feel grateful to Sam for struggling as far as the harbor before he let Toes call their parents. He reminded himself that Sam had hoped to surprise and please him by adding a finishing touch to the open-casket scene, Will's own special creation.

If I'd been there, Will said to himself, to help run the string over the curtain fixture. . .

But this morning he didn't feel quite so worried or guilty.

"I'm sorry," said Sam.

"Don't be," Will answered gruffly.

"I'm sorry for all of us. Do you think—do you think we should postpone the tour?"

"The invitations are out," Will replied shortly.

There was a solution. They had rehearsed enough to know each other's parts; Sam could lead the tour and Will could work behind the scenes.

Toes would suggest this sooner or later, Will felt sure, but he'd be ready for her. He'd tell her: We'll split the crew work and I'll do one of your performances, say, the casket scene. . . .

That would shut her up.

"So what do you think we should do?" Sam looked Will in the eye.

Will glanced away. "We still have four days."

75

"Yeah." He pulled himself up. "I'll practice on these sticks," he promised. "Who knows, my ankle could be much better tomorrow. I think it's feeling better already."

Toes is right, Will thought as he watched Sam hobble out the door: The kid's a lousy liar.

"What's today's special?" somebody shouted into the kitchen.

"Turkey."

"Boy, you're wearing thunderheads low as your earlobes," Winston said.

Will looked up from the tub of dishes he was carrying.

"What's wrong with you?"

"Nothing."

"Nothing. When kids are two they say *no*. When they're twelve they say *nothing*."

"And when they're forty-two they don't say you a thing," Will retorted. "They just ask a lot of questions."

"That's because they're curious," the cook responded.

Will pressed his lips together.

"And maybe they even care. You been mooning around this place for four days."

Will began to unload the dirty dishes.

"Slowing down out front?"

"No."

"So, let's live dangerously. Come outside with me. I want to show you what's in my pickup." The cook handed a long fork to a trainee. "Keep your eyeball on that bacon," he instructed. "It may look dead, but it's got its eye on you, and soon as you turn away it'll turn itself black."

The young man grinned.

When they got to the truck Winston pulled back an old gray blanket, revealing two small freezer chests. He lifted the lid of the first. "Three hearts, livers, necks, and gizzards. Two extra chicken livers from last week's special. Two greased sausages—" He shrugged. "Thought they might come in handy. Some moldy bread the missus was about to throw out this morning."

Will stared at the treasures, at once wishful and despairing.

Winston opened the next chest and Will reached inside for the lidded bucket. "Don't open it, not here, not in front of this nose. Edward went fishing last night. We got the fish, you got the cleanings."

Will picked up a jar of oozy yellow stuff, smiling when he realized what it was. "The devil! You saved some devil for me."

"Ought to be nice and foul by now," Winston said.

"Didn't refrigerate it and we had the crabs Friday. There's still room in here for your spaghetti and eggs. . . .

"Boy, I don't need to lecture you on respect for other people's property, do I?"

Will shook his head.

"This is one strange-looking picnic," Winston remarked, shutting the chests, pulling out a cigarette, looking at Will long and hard.

"You're going to die from those," Will said.

"That's a fact." Winston glanced down at his cigarette. "And that's an old trick, too old to distract an old father. You going to tell me why there's clouds hovering round your eyebrows?"

"No."

"Okay." The cook leaned back against his truck and drew on his cigarette. "So why don't you be forty-two?"

"What?"

"Ask me some questions. I'm ready for you."

Will considered. "What's the rottenest thing you've ever done to somebody?"

"No."

"What do you mean 'no'?"

"I'm not answering that question. Try again."

Will walked a circle around the truck, then asked, "Did you ever get mad at somebody for doing something—something sort of stupid—even though you knew he didn't mean to?"

"Yep. More than a few times. And I expect I'll get mad like that a few times again."

"So what if you were working on something with some other people and were really hoping to do something and everybody else hoped you would do it, too, and you knew you would be great at it and then something happens and the only way that that something could be done is if you let the person who made something go wrong, because he was trying to do something for you, do what you were going to do, which is the best thing, and you do his, which isn't much fun. What would you do?"

Winston rubbed his chin with his large hand. "I guess I'd do something."

"That's not an answer," said Will.

"It's as much an answer as I can give to that question. Why are we talking riddles when you're trying to figure something out?"

"Never mind," Will said, pushing off from the truck.

"Wait! Ask me again. Maybe I'll do better this time."

Will repeated the question, at one point getting himself lost in it.

"All right. I got it. The answer. It all depends."

"Winston!"

"Does the other person want to do the something you were going to do?"

"That's just it. He never says. Don't you think if he wanted the chance he should ask for it?"

"It all depends," the cook replied.

Will scowled.

"On whether that person thinks *you* really want to do the something. Maybe the other person doesn't want to ask for something that's so important to you. Maybe he's afraid you'll get mad or won't like him anymore."

"I'm already mad because if he wants a chance he should ask for it—fight for it!"

"Maybe he's waiting for you to offer it to him."

"Well, he's going to have to wait a long time! What should I do?"

"I don't know, Will."

"You're not helping me any."

"And I'll tell you why," Winston said. "Because I'm listening to you and thinking to myself you don't need my help. You already know a lot of answers, and I suspect, soon enough, you'll figure out which one is yours."

10
Opening Night

IT MIGHT WORK, WILL THOUGHT AS HE PASSED Sam, who was practicing on one crutch, trying to be silent, thumping around the house like the hunchback of Notre Dame. He would wait until the very last moment, when it would be too late for his neighbor to get nervous—or for himself to change his mind.

Earlier that evening the three had taken the town bus to Bridge Street. Sam had traveled quietly, speaking only once, to apologize for the fact that Will and Toes had to haul everything down the mainland road.

Toes had worried and chattered most of the way.

81

"Do you think if we have Sam set up the key spots, like the dining room, and skip some routines, such as the catsup bleeding from the upstairs hall, we could—but no, that's one of my favorite parts. . . . "

When they reached the house, Will raced about, hanging signs on the porch to direct their arriving guests and making last minute adjustments on the second floor. Meanwhile Sam oiled down Schaefer, and Toes put on a long robe and makeup.

"So," she said, her hair up on her head, her skin white as flour and eyes hollowed with violet shadow, "what if I push open the lid so Sam would have time to get to the dining room chairs and—"

Shouts from outside the house interrupted her.

"They're early! Will, this isn't going to work!"

They rushed together down the back steps.

"Don't touch the railing," he said.

"Eyah!"

"I told you."

Sam met them in the kitchen.

"You're on," Will announced.

The boy blinked.

"Where's your makeup, Toes?"

"Here."

"You remember the story," Will prompted as he dipped his fingers in the greasy stuff. "You want to do this . . . ?"

Sam nodded, his face bright.

"Say it," Will insisted. "Say it out loud."

"I want to do this."

The pounding on the back door grew more insistent. Will smeared shadow under Sam's eyes. "Now take off your shirt. Powder his head, Toes," he added as he unbuttoned his own top. They made the exchange, Sam's dark shirt for Will's light one, which, though a little long, fit Sam snugly across the chest and middle.

Removing his socks and tying them together with an old rag, Will wedged the bundle under Sam's tight collar, giving him a humped back. Then he took a step backward and looked the boy over. "You're not you, Sam. You're a servant left over from the good old days at the May Estate. Tell them the story that you know is true."

"Yes, sir," Sam replied, nodding and hobbling on one crutch, swinging his crooked body toward the back entrance. "Coming," he hollered. "Coming. Who be that pounding on Mr. May's door?"

Toes threw the makeup in the dumbwaiter, then, flashing a smile at Will, hastened toward her casket in the living room. Will positioned himself in the hallway, crouching deep enough in the shadows to be able to watch unseen. Sliding the bolt aside, Sam opened the back door and greeted the guests with a formal bow.

Jenko, Al, Ray, and Neal stared at him.

"We're looking for Willie Hanson," said Al.

"Willie Hanson." Sam mulled over the name. "When was he born?"

"What?"

"The year, sir," the courteous servant replied.

"What's this," Al sneered, "we got to answer riddles before we can get in the house? Seventy . . . uh . . . seventy . . . "

Will guessed that his schoolmate couldn't decide whether to add or subtract one from his own birth date.

"Don't know him," the hunchback said. "I died in '29."

Jenko laughed. "That's cool."

"If you are ready, gentlemen," their guide invited.

"I thought Willie-boy was going to be here."

"The invitation said *Mac*Han," Ray reminded Al.

"Right you are," said Jenko with increasing interest. "Wonder if that means sweet Sister Long-Legs is in on this."

Will hoped that Long-Legs, who by now should have been settled comfortably in her blackened vegetable crates, couldn't hear, lest the dearly departed rise in vengeance before her cue.

"So why don't we begin?" Neal asked, his voice echoing with a more hollow sound than the others'.

"Nervous?" Al laughed. "Just a teeny-weeny bit scared?"

Sam bowed to Neal. "I was waiting on you, sir," he said, and began the story of Ernest May, brother of the traitorous George, hunter, gambler, and bootlegger of the 1920s, famous for his large and often violent parties.

Will retreated to the billiard room and started the recording of a vicious animal (Schaefer), whose growls shifted into long, lonely howls.

Al warbled and mewed and oinked.

Why doesn't Sam stop the tour? Will wondered. He knew that Al would only get more out of hand; it would be best for Sam to make him leave now.

But the guide had another plan. As soon as the group left the kitchen, he turned off the flashlight.

Will heard the confusion as the boys bumped into the back hallway walls, attempting to follow Sam past the library into the billiard room.

"I can't see," Jenko complained.

"I can," Sam replied cheerfully. "This is the game room."

Al took out his Bic and snapped its end. Light flickered above a card table, burned along the metal of curved knives, then died. Al tried again. The boys glimpsed pictures of wild animals—a man killing a bear, a lion mauling a man.

Then Will pulled a string and a glass tipped, shattered. Al's light sputtered out—a special effect as good as any the trio had planned. From that point on, the tour sailed.

In the living room the casket opened slowly. Toes, having waited long enough to strain everybody's eyes and nerves, emerged with fangs bared.

An invisible crowd chattered (like restaurant customers) in the next room. "Smell it!" Neal said, backing away from the spread of fish innards and moldy bread.

A knife whistled past (Toes' aim suspiciously close to Jenko, Will thought). From the padded dining room chair came spurts of Heinz. Then shrieks (and a rattling like a roller-coaster track). One by one the off-balance chairs fell backward as Will pulled their connecting string.

In the kitchen raw eggs and crab gut oozed from the nostrils of George Washington. Hanging next to him, helping to conceal the opening of the dumbwaiter, was another presidential Paint-by-Number: Lincoln's eyes, as gray as Toes', followed the guests to the back steps.

As they climbed and tripped over stairway obstacles, the visitors' hands squeezed gizzards, hearts, and liver.

"A rat!" Ray called out. Everyone froze and the rodent rushed past (to a milkbone in the kitchen).

Upstairs they discovered a face, intestines—or was it worms?—floating in a darkened bath (four bottles of red and two bottles of blue). As the tour left the room Will rolled something in front of Al. "Sh—!" he cursed, stepping on the greased sausage.

Sam gambled in the master bedroom. When the guests noticed the dumbwaiter, he urged them away from it. Jenko felt compelled to shove the panel back.

She looked fantastic—dangling upside down from a hidden trapeze, her eyes rolled back in her head.

When it was all over, Will told her so.

"I know it," Toes replied. "I could feel it. Wish I could have seen myself," she added wistfully as they rode three across at the front of the Paradise bus. "The script was great. The props and timing perfect. We were all fantastic tonight, eh, Sam?"

Will leaned forward to look at the boy, who was sitting with his foot propped on Winston's ice chest. A smear of purple shadow was still visible beneath one eye. Will rubbed his own as a sign for Sam to do the same, but his neighbor didn't react.

"Hello, Sam."

The boy blinked, then, gazing back with clear eyes, smiled a little. "Hello, Will."

Before parting that evening, MacHan, Inc., launched its next project. In response to Ray and

Jenko's request for a second visit, the kids decided to offer a new, even longer tour, one that started after sunset and included the third floor. In addition to the original guests, the neighbors would each invite one new person and select one more by vote.

Sam reminded Will and Toes that in a week and a half his foot would be healed, so he could take a turn as crew.

Will fell asleep that night imagining himself holding eight people spellbound with tales of horror and crime.

11

More Choices

MONDAY AFTERNOON WILL RODE TO THE MAIN-
land, planning to stroll around the house, enjoy its
quiet, and come up with some new ideas for the
next tour.

It was raining, the kind of soft silver rain that he
especially liked. He rode on the shoulder of West
Road, deliberately running into the arms of shaggy
pines. The afternoon that the waitresses had called
"dreary" was really full of light, he noticed. Drops
of water rolled up the green-gray needles, beading
on them like mercury.

When Will arrived at the house he circled it,
surveying the windows on the second floor, won-

dering if any of the shutters could be worked open. Returning to his starting point, he walked swiftly toward the front porch and there was surprised to see a young man sitting with his back against the house, his long legs stretched out in front of him. Will noted the visitor's tan and, thinking his face familiar, wondered if he was one of the lifeguards who bought carryout from the diner.

"Hello." The blond-haired man greeted him with an easy smile, and Will now remembered seeing him about three weeks before, emerging from Mr. Wyeth's new trailer.

"Hi." Will's voice came out as a short blip. He was not happy to see this fellow relaxing against his house.

"Great place, isn't it?" the older boy said.

"Yeah."

"My name is Peter."

"Will," he replied with some reluctance, and stepped up on the porch.

"Careful where you walk. Any minute we could find ourselves three feet lower."

I know where to step! Will wanted to retort. "You live on the mainland?" he asked the young man.

Peter laughed. "On the mainland all right. In Baltimore. But this summer I escaped and am working at the marina, staying with my uncle, Henry Wyeth."

"Mr. Wyeth?" He's an old friend of my father's, Will was about to say, then stopped, afraid that word of their meeting here would get back to the diner. "You like boat work?"

"Better than restaurant work."

Will's back stiffened. "You can make a lot of money waiting tables."

"I know," Peter replied. "I've done it since I could walk. They tipped me with nickels and pats on the head. When you grow up in your parents' restaurant, you can't wait to get away from the pasta and silverware."

Will started to smile.

"I love ruins," the young man said, turning his head, laying his cheek against the house.

"So do I."

"This place must have a hundred stories to tell."

Will studied the visitor. Peter's mouth was gentle as a girl's, his nose strongly curved; it was a likeable face.

"You interested in stories?" Will asked.

"I write them."

"So do I. Well"—Will corrected himself—"I wrote most of one. The others, they're in my head, sort of like movies."

"You should put them down on paper."

"I know some good stories about this house," Will volunteered.

"True ones?"

"Uh, no . . ."

"That's all right. Tell me one anyway."

Will began the chain of tales given on the tour, improvising here and there.

Occasionally Peter stopped him. "You mean she was found dangling upside down in the dumbwaiter? Why? Who killed her? How come the murderer left her that way?" Will kept making up answers and the story grew more and more complex. He hoped he could remember half his great ideas.

When he had talked his audience all the way up to the cupola (it felt good to have the attention of someone who wasn't hoping for more coffee or catsup), Peter repeated, "You should write down these stories."

"Think so?"

"Sure," Peter said, and grinned. "You're a natural." Rising and stretching, he glanced at the front door, then reached for the handle. "Wish we could figure out how to get in this place."

"I know a way."

"You do?"

Sam and Toes would understand, Will told himself. If they met this guy, they, too, would want to give him a tour. "Follow me."

Inside the house Peter noticed things that others had not. He admired Will's handiwork on the back door. He complimented the "interior decorating" of the billiard room, noting the way the eye "skipped," as he said, from playing cards to flashing knives to pictures of wild animals. Had he been a little shorter, he would have tried out Toes' casket. He sat regally in the chair of death. Upstairs he tested the strength of the trapeze and laughed and stuck his hand in the tub of spaghetti. In the cupola Peter moved from window to window, exclaiming over the view, thanking Will several times for showing him the house.

"So why don't you be my guest on our second tour?" Will asked. "It's Thursday, June twenty-ninth. You'll be older than everybody else," he added, suddenly self-conscious. This guy was in college. Of course he wouldn't be interested in coming with a bunch of kids; he had been bored and was just amusing himself for the afternoon.

"What time?"

"Eight-thirty."

"I'll be there." Peter offered his hand.

After his guest left Will started to close up the house, bolting the stairway door from the inside and returning to the first floor via the dumbwaiter.

Maybe it'd be better not to tell Sam and Toes about this afternoon's tour, he thought to himself as he tucked up the rope ladder and set the false ceiling back in place. Not that he had done anything wrong—this wasn't what they meant when they promised—but he'd ask Peter not to mention the visit.

Will enjoyed one last stroll around the downstairs, reliving moments of last night's tour, imagining the next one with Peter as audience. Then he glanced at his watch. He'd have to stop over the marina another day—it would be fun to see Peter at his work—but for now, he'd better get back to Salisbury steak and silverware.

Tuesday morning Sam called an emergency meeting, but Will, who was hauling away mountains of dishes and pouring rivers of coffee into the cups of American Legionnaires, never felt the break between breakfast rush and lunch. Five minutes to three that afternoon he walked slowly toward the dock. There he stretched out and closed his eyes, letting the sun-warmed planks ease his back and legs.

"When you couldn't join us this morning—" Toes began.

Will sat up.

"I asked Sam to tell me what was wrong."

He glanced at Sam, who looked a little solemn.

"I haven't decided which one of you I'm going to kill first," said Toes.

Will pointed. "Him."

The boy started to grin and Will asked, "What's up, Sam?"

"Did you or did you not ask Al to be part of the second tour?" Toes demanded.

"I'm talking to Sam," Will replied, but then, as Toes' words sank in, he turned to her. "You mean, to come again?"

"I mean to be part of it. To join our team. To give the tour."

"Of course not."

"I told you!" Toes reproached Sam.

"He said that you did," the boy informed Will.

"He lied."

"I told you, Sam, I've told you a hundred times, just because you're honest, don't think everybody else is. Don't think *any*body else is."

"So," said Will, "did you let him know he couldn't?"

"I said if it was all right with you, it was all right with me."

"Sam! How could you be so stupid?"

The boy lifted his chin.

"You know I can't stand Al," Will continued.

"I don't know that," Sam replied quickly. "You never told me that."

"But it's obvious, he's a jerk!"

"It's obvious to me," Sam said, striding to the end of the plank walkway. "I didn't know if it was to you."

"What! Do you think I'm blind?"

"I thought"—Sam searched for words—"that even if you didn't like him, you might be afraid—"

"Of Al?" Will was offended.

"Of losing out with him."

"Well," said Toes, leaning over to pick up some stones, "looks to me like you have a choice, Will. You can be honest, for once. You can tell your *buddy* no, you don't want his help. Or, you can keep things cozy, and we'll all have the pleasure of his company." She skipped two pebbles across the water. "Tough choice," she said, and headed back to the grocery.

When she was gone, Will glanced at Sam. The boy had stopped pacing.

"You can't blame me for not knowing," he told Will. "You confuse me!" His voice grew quieter. "Sometimes you act like a friend. Sometimes you don't. I can't tell who you really like and who you're just pretending to get along with because you are . . . stuck with them. How am I supposed to tell when you're schmoozing and—"

"Schmoozing?!"

"Trying to keep things cozy."

Will turned away.

"So."

They stood at either end of the dock.

"Tell me when you decide," Sam said at last, and left.

Sighing, Will kicked a piling, then dropped down next to it, throwing his feet over the edge of the dock. He wished Randy was here. He wished it was last summer and his old friend was standing next to him, taking thirty-six pictures of Digger swimming.

Randy and he had known each other as far back as Will could remember, and they'd never once had to talk about being friends. They just were.

Schmoozing!

Lying back on the dock, Will stared up at the edgeless blue. It would be a long time, he thought, before he found a friend as fun and easy to be with as Peter. Maybe not until he got to college.

12
"Am I Talking to Will?"

WILL AWOKE THE NEXT MORNING—GRUMPY, TIRED from a night of tossing and turning—and put off every chore he didn't consider necessary. About seven forty-five, his father looked at him from across the diner and flicked his head toward the outside flagpole. Grudgingly Will fetched the banner from beneath the taffy and mint display.

As Will raised the flag, Al sped into the parking lot, skidded to a stop, and gave a mock salute.

Will, tied into his long apron and hoisting the Stars and Stripes in front of a sign that said 50 YEARS OF FAMILY DINING, felt like a picture on the back of a cereal box—"We're served at breakfast tables across the nation!"

Al squinted up at Will, smiled. He would remain genial, Will knew, as long as he thought there was a chance of getting what he wanted.

"You're around early," Will remarked.

Al sat back on his bike seat, his spine curved, his legs straight out like braces. "The old man was up early and making a lot of noise," he explained. "Came in late from last night's meeting. The morning after he always knocks things around."

Will nodded and wound the rope on the pole hitch. "Land breeze," he observed. "Flies today."

"So we're all set for the second tour?" Al spoke with but the slightest question in his voice. "When's our planning meeting?"

"What do you mean?"

"Didn't the kid—didn't Sam tell you? I'm helping out."

Will studied the boy's large, shiny face. "Who invited you?"

"He said if it was all right with you, it was all right with him."

"Well, it's not all right with me."

Al dropped back his head and looked at Will for a long moment. "I think I like the kid better than I like you."

Will shrugged. "He's a nice guy."

"You two sweet on each other?"

Will knew the s-word was carefully chosen.

"Are you pink?"

A strong protest would only encourage Al. "Like I said, he's a nice guy."

The boy feigned surprise. "Am I talking to Will?" he said, his voice breaking a little high. "Willie Hanson? Not the one I know. Not the one I like. You're changing."

"I know," Will replied wearily.

"*You know!* What the hell is that supposed to mean? I think you're pink."

"You're wrong," Will said, and started up the steps.

"Willie!"

At the door he turned to face Al.

The older boy leaned forward on the handlebars of his bike, as if he were waiting for Will to say something.

Will did not.

Al kicked his bike pedal twice around. "You're going to be sorry for this," he warned, then sped toward the street.

The following afternoon Will found Toes sitting at the curved end of the diner counter, well-positioned for people-watching. Every time he approached her, a customer or waitress hailed him, but Toes was as patient as she had been the first time she came to the diner. A surprising thought occurred to him: Maybe she needed breaks away from the grocery. Maybe she liked the sights and sounds of the diner.

"We'll have to take a detour to the house tonight," Toes said as soon as Will was within earshot.

"Hi, how are you?" he replied sociably.

One side of Toes' mouth curved up a little. "We told our parents we're going up on the boardwalk. So we'll have to look like it," she continued in a businesslike manner. "Is Al coming?"

"I figured you knew. I thought that was you at the window yesterday."

"It was. But there are a hundred things you could say that would make a person ride off mad."

Will matched her crooked smile, then took her order from the hands of a waitress. "Good choice," he remarked as he placed the dish before her.

"So what did you say?"

Will recounted the conversation, including Al's final threat. Toes listened quietly, uncurling a large onion ring, eating it with great delicacy. When Will finished, she said, "These aren't frozen, are they?"

"Fresh," he replied. "Winston's. Eight o'clock out front?"

"Yup." She sprang up from the stool.

"You want a bag for those, or are you going to wear them as bracelets?"

She hooped one over her narrow hand, then

snatched up the rest in a tuft of napkins. "Sometimes you're funny. . . . Not often," she called back across her shoulder.

Will was glad that Toes had come over. In some ways, he thought, she was easier to deal with, her bossy ways not nearly as hard to handle as Sam's silences.

"You know, Win, she's not so bad."

"Who we talking about?" the cook asked, looking up from a circle of dough. "*Not* Miss Toes!"

"Yeah, Toes."

"You and Missy MacDowell getting kind of friendly, aren't you?" remarked Mr. Dan, who had followed Will into the kitchen.

Will stepped free of the man's sweaty hand. "My father's back in the office," he said, with a nod in that direction.

After putting his thumb in the middle of Winston's pie crust, the man moved on.

"Why does Dad put up with him?"

Winston flipped over a clean juice glass, neatly excising the thumbprint. "Well, they went to school together, since first grade, your father always says."

"That's not a reason!"

Winston glanced up. "They grew up in the same town," he suggested.

"That's not either, not a good one."

The cook started to smile.

"Why are you looking at me that way?" Will asked.

"Tell me about Toes. Is she getting nicer, or are you?"

"Neither," he replied. "She says what she thinks. I do what I want to do. Neither of us wants to be friends, so nobody's got to worry about doing or saying the right thing. It's easy."

"Kind of freeing?"

Will watched the cook lay the pie crust in the pan and flute it with his knuckles.

"Yeah. Freeing."

"So just imagine, boy, what it's like when you don't worry about having to act one way or the other because you know somebody cares about you, somebody truly likes you for just the person you are." Winston spooned peaches into the pie crust. "I got a friend like that. We talk and do just the way we think. Of course, sometimes we've got to forgive each other. Sometimes we got to say I'm sorry."

Will leaned forward to scoop up a drip.

"But it's worth it," the cook continued. "It's a kind of friendship worth looking for, I think." He raised his eyebrows at Will. "Happens, you know."

"Yeah . . . "

Winston set down the bowl, smiling, and slapped Will lightly on the cheek. "Yeah!"

103

13

Enter: Who?

IN THE PINE WOOD SURROUNDING THE HOUSE IT was already night.

"Nice and gloomy," Will observed.

Sam, who had been thoughtful most of the way, suddenly spoke up. "What if we start the tour at the road? That way everybody will be in the mood before they reach the back door."

"With a few screeches and howls," Toes proposed. "Movement behind the trees."

"Something falling in their path," Will suggested.

"Bones," said Sam.

"Big enough to look human," Will added.

Toes nodded enthusiastically. "I'd kill for a skull."

"Well, that will get you one!"

104

Sam grinned. They were working as a team again, Will thought with relief. He opened the kitchen window and Toes and Sam followed him through.

When the outer shutters were closed, Toes flicked on her flashlight, then froze.

"Somebody's been here."

Will glanced around. "How can you tell?"

"The pictures—they're hanging crooked."

Sam straightened the portraits that hid the dumb-waiter, then turned suddenly and tiptoed to the stairway door.

"It's open," he whispered in disbelief.

"I thought we agreed to keep this bolted from the inside—"

"We did, we did," Will replied, waving her silent. He joined Sam, who was examining the bolt.

"Bent," the boy said in a hushed voice. "This door isn't going to shut anymore, not all the way."

"You were here Monday," Toes continued aloud.

"So?" Will mouthed to her.

"So, did you follow procedure?"

He hesitated. "I closed up the house as we always do."

Sam peered up the dark stairway, then stepped back, pushing the door closed as far as he could. "Do you think anyone else could be here now?" he asked quietly.

All three glanced upward, listening.

"So what if they are?" Toes' voice bounced off the walls. "We have as much a right to be here as anyone."

"As much right as anyone with no right," Will pointed out.

"Anybody home?" Sam hollered.

No reply.

"Let's check the first floor," he said.

Toes moved toward the dining room.

"Together." Sam raised his voice, and she turned around and followed the boys into the library.

The three of them played their flashlights over the walls and floor. Nothing appeared to have been touched, so they moved on to the billiard room.

"Cards." Toes pointed.

Two lay on the floor.

"We could have knocked them off."

"How many steak knives did you bring from the grocery?" Will asked.

"Two."

"I took four from the diner. Anyone see six?"

They searched the room for the missing knife.

"We may as well keep going," Sam said at last.

Will saw Toes slip one of the remaining knives in her back pocket as she left the room.

In the living room the lid of the casket gaped open, but nothing else was disturbed.

"Somebody was curious," Sam observed as they passed through the hall and into the dining room.

Will's light caught the corner of the table and he breathed out with relief when he recognized the narrow gleam.

"Well, at least no one is carrying it around upstairs," Toes said, picking up the steak knife. "A glass is missing. Two."

"Here—smashed." Sam directed his beam toward the kitchen doorway. On the floor shards of green sparkled.

"Freaking vandal," Toes muttered. "I wouldn't have thought Al was smart enough to find his way into the house," she added.

Sam shook his head. "This isn't Al's style. He would have left the place a mess."

"Maybe he's going to come back for more," suggested Toes. "Maybe he's going to destroy our house little by little"—she looked at Will—"to make us sorry, as he says."

Sam slid open the door of the dumbwaiter and shone his light upward. "You wouldn't have to be smart to find a way into the house," he said. "But who would have figured this was the way upstairs?"

Toes stuck her head in the shaft. "Someone who was careful to put the ceiling back in place," she noted.

Peter knew the way upstairs, Will thought uneasily.

The trio searched through the second and third floors. A chair was out of place, but nothing else appeared to be disturbed. Sam proposed that they take a careful look around the outside of the house. There they discovered one shutter forced loose on the old community window and hacking and kicking marks against the back door.

"See, it had to be someone who was part of our tour," Will said triumphantly. "Someone who tried the old way, and the tour entrance, then finally lucked out."

"Who else were we considering?" Toes asked.

For a moment he didn't have an answer. "Everyone."

She angled her head and looked at him long and hard.

This was not the time to tell them about Peter, Will said to himself. His confession would only muddle things.

"These marks are Al's style," Sam observed, pointing to the door, "but I think someone else got inside, someone with a different plan, some other purpose. That knife wasn't dropped. It was set down on the table."

"Yes, but the glasses," Toes reminded him. "They were—"

"Thrown," Sam suggested.

"At somebody!" Toes cocked her arm. "At somebody standing in the kitchen doorway!"

Her brother agreed. "What are you thinking, Will?"

"I . . . it's possible."

What plan could Peter have had? None, Will assured himself. The teenager had shown too much respect for their work to come back and smash glasses.

Reentering the house, Toes, Sam, and Will spent the next hour working on the upcoming tour. No one mentioned the break-in. Sam and Toes seemed to feel at home again, Will noticed, but he could not relax. As they walked through the scenes, he found himself glancing around the house, trying to find it—the clue—whatever it was that kept signaling him. Something was wrong.

14

Rumors

THE NEXT THREE DAYS WILL COULD NOT GET enough time away from the diner to check on the house. Sam and Toes were also busy, restocking shelves and bins emptied by the growing summer crowd.

When Mr. Hanson gave Will the thumbs-up sign Sunday evening, he hurried across the parking lot, a copy of the *Coastal Weekly* under his arm. In it, squeezed between ads for sailboat rentals and restaurants, was a letter to the editor from someone concerned about the preservation of old shore buildings, among them, the May house.

"Take a look at this," Will said, perching just below Sam on the steps that ran along the outside wall of the grocery. "All we need now is for the Historical Society to show up."

"Better them than bulldozers," Sam pointed out. "They probably wouldn't break anything."

"Yeah, well, we'd have a lot of explaining to do."

"You could manage that." Sam met Will's eyes, then, with a half smile, glanced down at the paper. "The letter isn't signed. I wonder why. Look here. Another fire at Mr. Wyeth's. People sure aren't happy with him."

"Not the fishing folk," Will agreed. "Let me see."

Sam held on to the paper. "He allowed them to investigate this one. Guess he's getting worried."

"Did they find anything interesting?" Toes asked, emerging from the door beneath the steps.

"A kerosene pool. They're calling it the work of an amateur arsonist."

Toes lifted her chin. "If I were Wyeth, I'd be insulted that they didn't send around professionals."

"According to this article, the blaze was discovered and reported by his nephew."

Will reached for the paper, but Sam held on to it, continuing to read.

"Did you tell Will what Ray said?" Toes asked her brother.

"When did you see Ray?"

"This morning." Sam handed back the *Weekly*. "The rumor is that Mr. Wyeth owns the land the

111

May house sits on. It seems someone knows someone who knows someone who was given the money
and a fee to buy the land for Mr. Wyeth."

"You mean the land and the house."

"No, not the house. That's what I can't figure."

"People do that," said Toes, "and then collect
ground rent from the person who owns the building.
They do it in Baltimore."

"It still doesn't make sense to me," Will replied.

If Peter knew, wouldn't he have said something?
Will recalled as much as he could of his conversation
with the young man. He had never even hinted that
his uncle owned the land. Will had shown him
everything, told him all that he and Sam and Toes
were doing, but Peter had not been so open with
him. Will felt as if he had been deceived.

How will Sam feel, he wondered, when I tell him
my secret?

"Ray said Al went up to his grandmother's on Kent
Island," Toes told Will. "Last Monday. So that elim-
inates him as suspect. Who else might have been
fooling around in our house?"

Not Peter! Will thought, rolling up the *Weekly*
tight as a stick. Peter wouldn't have broken anything.

"Is something bothering you?" she asked.

Will jumped up. "Nothing is bothering me!"

Sam looked at Will with one eyebrow raised, and Will stared back at him. The boy did not blush, he noticed. And he was acting pretty cool about the visit from Ray, almost as if he expected it.

Now that Sam was so sure of himself, what did he think of Will? If he found out about Peter's tour before Will told him, what would he say?

I'll tell him everything tomorrow, Will promised himself. Or the day after. By the end of the week, for sure.

Trudging back to the diner, Will could feel Sam's eyes in his back.

15
Look Again

WILL HAD JUST FINISHED THE CHORES OF THE morning shift and was zipping three cans of spray paint into his knapsack when Wednesday's mail arrived.

"Package for you, Willie," a waitress called into the kitchen. "At the cash register. Your mom said it's from Washington."

As soon as he saw the taped-up box, Will knew it was from Randy. He stuffed the parcel in his knapsack, jumped on his bike, and pedaled to the house, where Sam and Toes were already at work.

Will had been hoping to hear from Randy, wishing for a postcard. It seemed unlikely that his friend would send a long letter, for he had never been a writer. Will guessed that the package was full of photos and wanted to view them in private. He'd open it at the house.

When he arrived there, Sam and Toes were not in sight. Hoping that they had already begun the afternoon's project on the third floor, Will walked as quietly as possible across the kitchen toward the billiard room.

Sam intercepted him at the hall door. "I didn't hear you come in."

"Was anything messed up?" Will asked.

"No, but Schaefer is acting funny."

"What d'you mean?"

"He's sniffing a lot and walking around in circles."

Will could hear the dog's tags jingling in the front hall, then the dining room. As he passed the boys Schaefer took a whiff of Will, then continued on past the library and back up the hall again.

"It's the same path over and over," Sam said, his eyes dropping down to Will's package.

"Looks as if he's tracking something," Will observed.

"I know, but the only things he's ever tracked are dogs and squirrels. It's not likely that either of them pried open the kitchen window."

"No . . ."

"What's that you're carrying?"

Will rotated the package so that the return address showed. "Pictures, I think, from Randy, my friend who used to live where you do."

Sam was silent for a moment. "Are you going to open it?"

"Sure."

"Here?"

"Sure," Will repeated, turning the package one way, then the other.

"A steak knife will cut that tape," Sam suggested.

"Good idea," Will replied without moving.

Sam suddenly stepped past Will. "I—I'm going up to the nursery, to help Toes. Call me if you want . . . anything."

"It's really no big deal," Will said. "You can look at the pictures."

The boy turned and studied Will's face. "I'll be around a little later," he replied.

When Sam had disappeared, Will fetched a knife from the billiard room, then hurried up the back stair, thinking how pleased Randy would be to know that his pictures were viewed in the cupola. On the third floor, Will tiptoed past the room where Toes was setting up demonic toys. She stuck her head out the door, but Sam's hand reached through and pulled her back, and Will continued up the spiral stair.

116

With sweaty hands he cut the tape, tore paper, slit a seam, and pulled open the flaps. Inside the box he found three envelopes of photographs and a short note: "We won't be coming down to Paradise for a while. Here are some pictures. Hope you like them. How is Digger?" Will winced.

In the thinnest pack was a series of colored pictures taken in December. Will and Digger stood on the dock, a mist of purple-blue, bay and sky, all around them, a string of Christmas lights twinkling from the marina across the way. Digger trotted close to the camera, snow and mud on his nose. Will and Randy's faces, almost gold, filled a picture. Randy, standing alone outside the grocery, looked straight into the camera, his face thinner, the angle of his jaw sharper than Will remembered. Will put that photo at the bottom of the pile and looked again at the picture of the two of them.

The second envelope was stuffed with curling black-and-white photographs, which Will guessed Randy had developed and printed himself. Labeled "Easter Sunday," they were the pictures his friend had taken the last time he visited Paradise, during spring break.

The first eight-by-ten caught Will by surprise. Bits and pieces of trash, snared by a circular wind, swirled between a boarded-up guesthouse and an abandoned popcorn stand; at the bottom of the picture, garbage collected around a police barrier. Will laid the print on a window seat, then dealt out the rest of the photographs, studying each one before he placed it on a bench, working his way around the square cupola.

Reverend Taub stood off-center, squinting into harsh spring sunlight, his long, lean body casting a bent shadow against the church door. Parishioners, with arms wrapped around themselves, pressed together in their light-colored clothes. Larry Harper, the only one who didn't look cold, stood with his hands in his pockets, his back to the crowd. Will wondered what kind of lens his friend had used for Mrs. Danson. Her nose and a large lily, growing front center on her hat, pressed close to Randy's camera, her heavy cheeks spreading back to the left and right, her pencil smile reminding Will of a graphed curve moving toward infinity.

With a telephoto lens Randy had foreshortened the boardwalk's Easter parade, so that the people of the town appeared to stand on one another's heels. Next to the parade queen, a teenage marcher glared into the camera with one eye, half of her face covered by whipping hair.

Randy had worked his way down the promenade to the amusements, where people posed in front of funny mirrors, stretching and twisting in response to their own distorted images. There was only one photo of the ocean, a view of the breaking surf channeled by the long, dark shadow of the pier.

Will had been with his friend the entire day he shot the pictures, but now he walked around the cupola several times, staring at his private exhibit as if he had never seen these scenes before.

He was reaching for the envelope of Kodachrome prints when Sam called from the foot of the stair, "Can we come up?"

"Uh, sure."

Toes preceded her brother, and as soon as she reached the top of the stair began picking up the black-and-white photographs. Moving out of her and Sam's way, Will sat down on the steps, dangling between his knees the envelope of Kodachromes and the third photo packet, still sealed. He wasn't sure he wanted to see anymore.

"These aren't tourist pictures, that's for sure," Sam remarked after the first full round. "They're not postcards."

"This guy is good," said Toes. "I mean, really good."

Sam picked up the picture of Mrs. Danson and her infinitely stretching lips. "What kind of lens is this?" he asked his sister.

"A fish-eye, a very wide angle lens."

The boy set it down and made another round of the pictures, then turned to Will. "What do you think of these?"

Will shrugged.

"Do they bother you?" Sam asked.

"Yes."

"They were meant to," Toes said matter-of-factly. "This guy knows what he's doing. I kind of wish I had met him."

Will handed her the photograph from the bottom of his pile.

Sam peered over Toes' shoulder. "Does this look like Randy?"

"Not the way I remember him."

"I'd like to see the rest of the pictures," Toes said.

Will gave them to her.

"Digger," Sam exclaimed softly as Toes sorted through the Kodachromes. "Where were you, Will, on the dock?"

"In a dream world," Toes observed. "He's got *you* pegged right!"

She flipped through the pictures again and Sam pulled out the one of Will and Randy by the light of the Christmas tree. "Is this how you remember him?"

"I guess," Will mumbled as he rose to his feet. "I'm going to start painting the master bedroom.

Leave the pictures on the seat when you're finished."

A few minutes later, Sam joined Will downstairs. "You miss him, don't you?"

"Who?"

"Randy. Digger, too."

"Stand back," Will warned, shaking a can of spray paint and sending swirls of black up the wall.

"I guess nobody likes things to change," said Sam.

Will turned quickly. "I expected things to change, to change this summer. But I thought last winter would always be the same. I didn't think somebody could make things you remember look different."

"Maybe the kinds of things you remember are in this pack of pictures," Sam suggested, picking the envelope up from the floor. "Did you look?"

"No."

"I'd like to."

Will shrugged and Sam slid his finger beneath the glued manila leaf. "They're photographs of our house," he said.

Will shook his can of paint and pointed it at the wall.

"They're good," Sam said. "They're great!"

Will glanced over his shoulder.

"Hey, Toes!" Sam hollered. "Come see. What's this, are you the ghost?" He held up the picture.

Reluctantly Will stepped closer, then, recognizing the shot, broke into a slow smile. "It turned out, just like he said it would!"

He explained to Sam how Randy had steadied the camera with a tripod and left the shutter open long enough to produce a clear picture of the front entrance and a blurred image of Will moving from the door toward the camera.

Toes, who had scurried down the dumbwaiter, reached over her brother's shoulder for the print. As she studied the picture her face grew serious. "Something's not right here. There is something different about the door."

"Looks the same to me," said Sam.

"It's not," she insisted. "The door itself . . . the lock! That's not where the padlock is now."

Sam examined the picture a second time, then started for the back stair. Will and Toes followed, Toes racing around the outside of the house and reaching the front porch first. She stood there breathless, waving the photograph, pointing at the door.

"Well, you were right," Sam said. "Were these pictures taken at Easter, Will?"

He nodded.

"Do you think a change of lock means a change of owner?" Sam suggested.

"It means at least this much," answered Toes. "Someone can and probably did get in our house through the front door. And there's no way we'll be able to stop that person."

"Especially if he's the owner," Sam remarked wryly. "I wonder if he was surprised to find his house already interior decorated."

Toes rolled and unrolled Will's ghost photograph. "You can bet he wasn't pleased."

"But he didn't leave any messages telling us to get out," Sam noted, reaching for the photo that Toes was curling, returning it to Will.

"And that's almost permission," Toes said, jumping off the porch.

As they headed toward the back door, Sam dropped back to walk beside Will. "You know, sometimes places or people I liked have changed," he said slowly. "But sometimes, I just thought they did. Because I saw a part of them I never noticed before. They're still them, but they're . . . more . . . more than I knew they were. Know what I mean?"

"Maybe," said Will.

16

An Uninvited Guest

THURSDAY MORNING WILL PEDALED OVER TO THE mainland with two thoughts in mind: to remind Peter of that evening's tour, and to ask him not to mention his private one.

Will had planned to confess to Sam and Toes yesterday, but could not find the words. Just as well, he thought now as he turned into the marina; he'd wait until tonight when they were celebrating their huge success.

After locking his bike to a post, Will checked the leased slips and the sailboat rental and tack shop, but there was no sign of his friend. He wandered about for twenty minutes, then approached a young

124

man and woman who were working dockside gas pumps.

"Peter?" The fellow responded to Will's question with a scowl. "Wyeth's nephew? He doesn't work here."

"He told me he did."

"Not anymore."

Will studied the attendant. Though dressed in khakis and a polo shirt, like Baltimore boat people, he spoke with a local accent.

"Where does Peter work now?" Will asked.

The young man flicked his head toward the girl operating the next pump. "Ask Kim. She should know." He raised his voice. "She was sure taken with Peter, Peter Wyeth Mancini. Kim, where's your friend and mine, our hardworking fellow employee? He must've left you his forwarding address, or maybe his telephone number so you can chat him up long distance."

The girl frowned at the older boy, then told Will, "He went back to Baltimore. This morning."

"To Baltimore!"

"That's right. His parents have a restaurant there."

"But he hated it," Will protested.

She cocked her head.

"Guess he hated it here even more," the older

boy said with a smile that said *You fool.*

Silently, Will backed away from the smirking attendant and tripped over a dock plank.

Maybe he didn't know Peter as well as he thought.

"It still smells like paint in here," Toes said that evening as they dropped their knapsacks in the May house kitchen. "Did you throw away the newspapers?" she asked Will.

"I took them and the rags and the cans home with us. And"—he unpacked the fish eyes, letting them shine a minute beneath his flashlight— "you asked me that twice yesterday."

"With the house closed up all the time, the fumes don't get much chance to escape," Sam observed.

Toes continued to shake her head and sniff. "The smell's too strong," she said, opening the door to the back stair, where she stored her makeup and the vegetable oil for Schaefer's rat look. She reached in, then turned back quickly, holding up an aerosol can. "Perhaps I should have asked you *three* times."

Will stared at the paint container in amazement.

"Maybe you didn't bring all of them?" she prodded.

"We had only three to begin with," Will protested. "And all three—"

She reached in again and a moment later threw a bundle of rags onto the kitchen floor.

Will's mouth dropped open.

Sam frowned.

"I told you these could start a fire," Toes said.

"But I didn't—"

"Set them outside the house," Sam directed.

"I'm telling you I didn't—"

"It's getting late," Sam interrupted. "I'll put the alcohol lamp in the cupola and light the candles on the first and second floor. You and Toes get dressed and—"

"But I didn't leave them! You believe me, don't you, Sam?"

"You better get dressed now," he answered mildly, "and set up the food props."

Toes swooped up the rags and carried them out the back door, still shaking her head. As soon as she and Sam disappeared Will went to look at the stairway. Certain that he had taken everything home, he felt at once embarrassed and outraged by their assumption.

Of course, what else could they think?

And I haven't admitted the one thing I'm really guilty of, Will thought.

The stairway retained the distinct smell of the paint rags. Who had been using them, he wondered, and why?

Dressed now in his white shirt, Sam's dark jacket, and Toes' bow tie, Will reddened his lips and hol-

127

lowed his eyes, then smoothed vegetable oil into his hair.

"She's taking an awfully long time out there," he said half to himself, half to Schaefer, who was nervously trotting around the kitchen.

"Will! Toes! Come quick."

Will ran to the back door and shouted to Toes, then hurried up the steps, Schaefer at his heels.

He found Sam in the front bedroom, standing two feet back from the window, a chunky silhouette against the darkening sky.

"Put out your flashlight," the boy said quietly.

Will flicked it off.

"Somebody's out there. Not a kid. He was standing at the edge of the clearing—must have been watching the house. I surprised him when I opened the outside shutter."

Will stepped closer. "Did you get a good look at him?"

"No."

"I did," Toes said as she entered the room. "Why do you suppose Mr. Wyeth is sneaking around property that he is supposed to own?"

Sam and Will looked at each other.

"Maybe he's hoping to be invited on the tour," Toes suggested, one side of her mouth twisting up. "I wonder how he knew it was tonight."

Peter told him, Will thought, sinking back against the wall. He went and told his uncle everything.

Toes shone her light into Will's face. "What do you know that we don't?"

Had this been the beginning of June, Will would have retorted, "A lot!" Now he glanced miserably from her to Sam.

"I don't think I want to hear this," Sam said quietly.

"I do," responded Toes.

"As a matter of fact," Will began, "I . . . uh . . . have been meaning to tell you something. Every time I see you I've meant . . . to tell you something."

They waited.

"I gave a tour, once, when you weren't here. I— He was sitting on the porch one day, when I had come over to work on the house. He was kind of friendly, real interested in the house. I . . . didn't think you'd mind."

"You gave a tour to Wyeth?" Toes asked incredulously.

"No! No, to Peter. Mr. Wyeth's nephew. You remember him," Will hurried on, "the real nice guy, curly-haired, who came out of the trailer when—"

"I remember," said Sam.

There was a long silence. Toes began walking in

129

a circle. *"Why* am I surprised? Why?" Turning on her heel, she left the room.

"I didn't think you'd mind," Will said to Sam. "I mean, if you had talked with Peter then you probably would have . . . " Will's voice betrayed his doubt.

"I don't care so much that you showed him around," Sam replied. "But I can't believe you didn't tell us afterwards. And you still didn't say anything when we had the trouble."

Will nodded unhappily.

"We were all trying to figure out what was going on, and you just played along!"

"But I didn't think it was him. I was sure it wasn't."

Sam turned away and started poking candles into soda bottles, arranging them on a wooden box.

"Sam, I'm sorry."

Glancing at his watch, Sam said without enthusiasm, "It's almost time. You better finish up the prop work so we can get on with this."

17

"Something Smells"

CONCENTRATE! WILL SAID TO HIMSELF. THAT'S what the best athletes did—put their mistakes behind them.

Concentrate. For the next half hour you're Mr. May's butler.

At the moment, it was a relief to be anybody but himself.

As Will made his way through the pines he mentally reviewed his script. He wanted this to be the best performance of his life. If he succeeded, maybe all would be forgiven.

While still within the wood Will spotted the gathering guests: Neal; Jenko; Ray and Ray's younger cousin, George, up from Roanoke; Sam's guest, a summer-condominium kid named Charles; and Lucy, a girl who would be in Toes' class next fall. Al hadn't shown yet, though Jenko said he was back in town. If he didn't come in time, Will planned to bolt the kitchen door behind the guests.

He wished that Edward had arrived. Winston's nineteen-year-old son had been everyone's choice as an extra guest. Will had hoped that he and Peter would enjoy each other's company, but now he wondered if Edward, too, would let him down.

I'll give him two more minutes, Will thought, and moved a little closer to the road to watch Jenko watch yellow-haired Lucy, who was attentive to Ray.

Will was about to give up when he heard the sound of a car motor. He had come! Six feet two inches eased out from behind the steering wheel of an old Dodge. The young black man waved. "Hi, guys."

From the passenger side Al emerged. His late start had paid off: He walked jauntily, as if he had been cruising around with the older boy.

Will waited until Edward had shaken hands with everyone, then, thrusting aside the underbrush, stepped before the guests. "Good evening, gentlemen, and lady." Will bowed. "The family awaits you. Kindly follow."

132

They did, Neal and Charles on Will's heels, then Lucy with Jenko close behind, and Ray and his cousin. Al hung back. Glancing over his shoulder, Will was glad to see Edward gesture for the boy to precede him, so graciously that Al could not refuse.

Choosing an indirect route to the house, Will walked with the beam of his flashlight low to the ground, letting the gloom and sudden coolness of the wood envelop his guests. An animal whined. Everyone looked to the left and Will slowed down, walking a few steps backward. A half minute later something howled and everyone spun to the right. Toes was fast, Will thought, and better at it than Schaefer.

The group moved on, alert but quiet, until the mosquitos found them and everyone started slapping arms and legs. Now, Toes, Will thought—before the mood is lost!

Objects hurtled through the trees.

"Heads up!" shouted Ray's cousin.

"Don't mind the bones," the butler said, and calmly walked on. Glancing back he saw the guests searching the underbrush. Edward stood apart, looking at him with an appreciative sparkle in his eyes. Will started to feel better.

He watched with pleasure when Al straightened up, wielding high above his head two large ribs and a shank bone. ("You making soup, or a person?" Winston had joked.)

Jenko asked if he could carry one of the trophies and, in an unusually generous mood, Al handed the second rib to Neal. The group marched on.

As they walked up on the southwest porch, the back door mysteriously swung inward.

"Ohhh!" gasped Lucy, taking a step backward.

Jenko was ready for her.

Standing by the door like a courteous butler, Will waited for the group to enter the house before him. Then, as he drew the door closed, he saw it—a flash of light among the trees, something that grew bright, then dimmed almost instantly. Will hesitated, reluctant to shut the door until he knew what he had seen. The guests standing behind him grew restless in the dark. Feeling uneasy, he pulled the back door all the way closed and bolted it.

Will soon discovered how difficult it was to guide so many people down a dark, narrow hall. The guests stumbled and bumped their way into the billiard room and, on the way out, someone knocked into the table of knives. Two slid to the floor with a clatter.

Al picked up one. Will took it from him immediately. "Mr. May will not be pleased," the butler said, then stooped to retrieve the knife that had fallen further under the covered table.

At first Will couldn't believe his eyes: paper food containers and paint rags were piled beneath the furniture. Who left these here? he wondered. Will thought of Toes' warning. What if there had been a candle on the table?

He stood up slowly and faced the guests, who looked back at him curiously. Will urged them on, despite his growing anxiety.

When he saw the flock of votive lights surrounding Toes' casket, he drew back. His response was contagious. Will wished he could enjoy everyone's imaginary fear. He wished he could tell Toes to blow out the candles before she came upstairs.

The group watched spellbound as the dead rose and walked. When she slept again and the casket lid dropped shut, George turned to his older cousin. "Something smells, Ray. Really smells."

"Don't mind the embalming fluid," the butler said.

In the dining room a knife whistled past, chairs fell back and Sam, passing behind Will, whispered, "Kerosene. The drape by the casket is soaked."

"Candles out," Will hissed, but Sam had already moved on to his next post. Will wished he hadn't bolted shut the house's main exit. Though they passed the back door again, he couldn't think of a way to unlock it and stay in character. He led the group up the turning stair.

From the top Sam released slicked-down, rat-faced Schaefer, who carried a turkey heart in his mouth and, with perfect instinct, dropped it on the foot of Ray's cousin. The boy picked it up, then threw the slimy muscle forward. It was caught by Jenko. "Gross!" He flipped the meat to the back of the line.

Will ushered the group through the hall to the bathroom. As everyone ogled the floating face, Will felt a finger in his back.

"You couldn't be this stupid," Toes said.

Her hand flashed open and Will stared down at a marijuana joint.

"There's more stashed in the dumbwaiter, and these—"

In a Kleenex she held four shiny packs of diner matches.

"Somebody's going to burn this place—Al!" She almost spoke aloud.

Will stopped the boy just as his fingers brushed the water.

The next stop was the master bedroom. Will took the group on a circuitous route, giving them plenty of time to look out the unshuttered window so that Toes could make it back to the dumbwaiter.

In the master bedroom even the original guests were temporarily disoriented by the black diagonal swirls that swept up the wall—like scorch marks, Will thought. Then Jenko took over and baited Lucy as Sam had baited the others before.

Will watched as if he were viewing a movie in which he was an actor, as if he were, at once, inside and outside the scene. Should he stop the show now? he wondered. Was the group in danger? Arsonists aren't murderers, Will told himself. Nobody will try anything while we're in here.

As they climbed higher and further away from the house's exits, Will talked faster. But the guests, delighted to have made it to the third floor, resisted his effort to hurry them along.

When they reached the door to the cupola's stair, Will stood in front of it, gesturing them ahead, hoping no one would notice its frame in the dim light. Edward might have. After he passed he ran his finger along the wall, then turned back to look at Will.

Will blinked. The young man's face was so much like his father's. For that moment his eyes were Winston's, searching Will with a mixture of curiosity and worry.

With relief Will finally escorted the group downstairs. Still playing the part of the butler, he thanked them all for coming and bid them a fine good-night.

18

In the Dark

THE MOMENT WILL CLOSED THE BACK DOOR TOES
emerged from the dining room. "They're going to
burn this place down."

Sam pushed through the back stair door. "We've
got to go for help."

"But somebody should stay," Will said.

"Only if you want to fry in—embalming fluid,"
Toes replied.

"I don't think they'll do anything as long as we're
here," Will told her. "They've held off this long."

She shook her head. "I wouldn't put anything past
Wyeth."

"What makes you so sure he's to blame? Maybe

he's just a spectator," Will argued, "and the people who set his boat and boathouse on fire—"

"Maybe he set the first two fires," Toes replied.

"Why?" asked Sam.

"To collect insurance, to . . . to . . . " She looked annoyed at her brother for asking the question. "When I know I'll tell you."

"And why tonight, with us around to witness?" Sam persisted. "He probably knew about the tour from Peter."

Will bit down on his lip.

"Of course he did," Toes said with exasperation. "Peter ratted and Uncle Wyeth saw his big chance. So guess who's getting framed?" She stretched open her pocket, which was filled with matchbooks advertising the diner. "Even without these, Wyeth will get away with it. Eight guests and the three of us are going to have to come up with alibis for where we were tonight. You can be sure that one out of the eleven is going to slip up—or tell the truth."

Both she and Will looked at Sam.

"We've got candles here, an alcohol lamp," Toes continued. "We've been painting. . . ."

Will slumped against the wall. "I played right into his hands. I got us set up."

"You sure did," she snapped.

"We're wasting time," Sam reminded. "You're the fastest, Toes."

She started toward the door.

"I'll wait here until you come back with help," Will said.

"Fetch Schaefer," she directed. "Put out the candles and the lamp and close—what do you mean you'll wait?"

"They won't do anything as long as I'm here."

"Don't be an idiot, Will."

"I'm telling you—"

"I'll stay with him," Sam volunteered. "If there's any sign of trouble, we'll get out."

"You know, I'd like to admire you two, I really would, but you're naive. You're just so—" She threw up her hands, then rushed out the door.

Will turned to Sam. "I think we should leave the lamp in the cupola lit as a sign we're still here."

After making certain that all the candles were extinguished and tying Schaefer to a tree at the edge of the wood, the boys returned to the house.

Will led the way into the dining room. Under the sweep of his flashlight the long table glittered: green glassware, diner plates, Mrs. MacDowell's old candlesticks. "When Toes comes back with help, we're going to have a lot of explaining to do," he remarked.

"I know—I can handle that."

Kicking at the string that connected the chair legs,

he broke it, then pulled back a chair and sat down. Sam took a seat across from him. They both stared down at the moldy bread and fish cleanings.

"It stinks in here." Will rubbed his nose.

"You were great tonight," said Sam.

"Think so?"

"Know so."

"Does that mean everything is . . . uh . . . okay between us?"

"That means you were great tonight," Sam replied.

"I thought it was a nice way of saying—"

"I can't trust you, Will."

"I don't know what to do about it," Will replied helplessly.

"You lie to me as easily as you would to Al, as easily as you'd schmooze with a diner customer."

"I don't schmooze! Do I?"

Sam didn't reply.

"Maybe you could give me one more chance."

"Maybe you could ask me later?"

Will shrugged. "Sure."

The boys lapsed into a long silence.

Sam rested his chin on the head of his flashlight. Will shone his downward. He didn't feel like seeing. "We're going to lose this place," he said at last.

"I think it means more to you than me," Sam

replied, raising his head a little. "I mean, the house itself means more. I guess you spent a lot of time here before I came."

"I just keep losing." Will's voice got stuck in his throat. "One thing after another. I just keep losing." Rising abruptly, he circled the first floor once, twice, then sat down again.

Sam watched him, but said nothing.

"Do you think we should check the lamp again?" Will asked.

Sam glanced toward the two outside walls of the room, then turned his head as if he heard footsteps close to the house. "Did it have much alcohol left when you checked it before?"

"I thought *you* checked it."

They looked at each other, then jumped up simultaneously and ran for the back steps. When they pulled open the third-floor door, the spiral stair was in darkness.

"Oh, no."

"How long do you think it's been out?" Will asked.

"There's no way of— Did . . . you . . . did you hear something?"

They stood very still.

"Maybe it's Toes," Will said, though he doubted she'd be back so soon. Removing his shoes, he tiptoed to the top of the back stair. Sam followed.

"ANYBODY HOME?"

The boys froze.

"Anybody home?" the man hollered again.

Sam moved close to Will. "Do you recognize his voice?"

Will nodded. "Wyeth."

"Should we answer?"

"Yes. No. We know this place better than he does," Will whispered, snapping off his flashlight. "We should be able to get around him."

Sam looked doubtful, but he removed his shoes and followed Will down to the second floor.

"Will? Sam? Toes?" Mr. Wyeth shouted. "Am I too late for a tour?"

The man's heavy footsteps sounded directly beneath them as he made his way across the kitchen, then paused.

"He's looking for the rags," Will said.

They heard Wyeth curse, then the first step creak beneath his weight. Will and Sam hurried around the corner into the master bedroom.

"There's no other place," Sam said, sliding back the panel to the dumbwaiter.

"Will the ladder hold both of us?"

"I'll up, you down," the boy proposed.

"You down, I'll up," Will replied, knowing his neighbor was less agile than he.

With an extra boost from Sam, he pulled himself onto the trapeze in a sitting position. Then he stood with feet spread apart on the horizontal bar, steadying himself by grasping one of the suspension lines and a safety rope that dropped from the third floor. Meanwhile, Sam climbed over the sill and eased the panel shut behind him.

"Get down further," Will called hoarsely. "Further."

Sam's foot had just touched the fifth rope rung when the panel slid back. A beam of light shone straight in between the boys. Will held his breath. The light swung away and back, and the door closed again.

Wyeth's footsteps continued around the second floor, pausing in one of the bedrooms.

The boys strained their ears.

"What's that noise?" Will whispered.

After a moment Sam replied. "Bottles. He must be moving some of the candles in the front room."

"Sounds as if he's carrying them downstairs."

"Probably," Sam said matter-of-factly. "Fire burns up."

They could hear the man on the first floor now, dragging something across the front of the house.

"When can we get out of here?" asked Sam.

"As soon as he does. . . . Fire burns up," Will

144

repeated. "That's going to make it awfully tough getting down."

Sam said nothing.

"What do you think Wyeth would do if we called out now?"

Sam remained silent.

"Maybe we don't have to face him," Will continued. "If we climbed out and waited at the top of the stair, we could run right down when—Sam, are you listening?"

"I'm listening. I'm thinking."

"I'm sorry, Sam, about this mess."

"What?"

"I said I'm sorry."

Sam's voice broke as if he wanted to shout at Will. "Why do you confess whenever you get in here?"

"Because I feel like I'm going to die," Will huffed back.

The walls of the chute vibrated.

"He's below us," Will whispered.

Sam scrambled up three rungs.

The first-floor panel slid back and Mr. Wyeth's light shone into the bottom corner of the dumbwaiter. "Kids," he muttered. "Having a good time tonight."

Will guessed he had been looking for the marijuana and matches.

Wyeth piled litter in the bottom of the compartment. Will watched anxiously. The next instant he saw it, a flame no bigger than a fingernail, drop into the trash.

Sam reached up quickly to slide back the panel.

"Go!" Will urged, readying himself to swing down behind the boy. But the fire blew up immediately and Will, drinking down a stomachful of black smoke and fumes, momentarily lost his balance.

Pulling Will by his legs, Sam dragged him through the opening and threw him on the floor, rolling him over several times.

"I'm okay," Will choked. "Okay."

With Sam's help he stumbled to his feet, then pulled his shirt up over his mouth. Unable to speak, he reached toward Sam and yanked the boy's T-shirt up to his nose.

The heat roared through the chute, driving the boys from the room. On the floor below them, Will saw flames shoot along a path of debris.

Sam pointed across the hall to the bedroom where the shutters had been opened. Will nodded: better to try the porch roof than risk being trapped in the kitchen stairway.

But smoke engulfed them before they reached it. Will stood still, flicking on and off his useless flashlight. He could see fires burning below, but could not get his bearings.

146

He reached out for Sam and the two of them groped their way across the stairless hall. If one of us steps over, Will thought, we'll both fall.

At last his hand touched the doorway. He pulled Sam in behind him, then saw the thing ignite—the candles had been moved close and tipped—the window frame curled back with flame.

Black smoke filled Will like a poison. He coughed uncontrollably.

"Get down," shouted Sam. "Down!"

The air was clearer close to the floor, but the boards were hot. Sam reached back and put Will's hand around his own ankle, then started crawling toward the kitchen stair. Will tried to crawl, felt himself being dragged along the crackling floor.

Time stretched till he knew no time, then he started falling, tumbling down steps. He heard shouting. He heard his name, Sam's name, being called. He felt himself being pulled, then carried by someone stronger than Sam.

And then he felt sand and strands of grass wet against his cheek.

19

Another Chance

"THANK GOD. I JUST THANK GOD," HE HEARD MR.
Wyeth saying over and over.

Will struggled to sit up. "Sam? Where's Sam?" It
was hard to talk without coughing. "Where's—?"

"Sam's okay," the medic said. "Be still."

A small round light was shone in one eye, then
the other.

"We're checking out okay," the medic called over
her shoulder.

As Will's eyes began to focus he saw his mother
standing close by, Winston's big hands capping her
shoulders. His father stood next to her like a block
of wood, everything still but the liquid rims of his
eyes.

West Road was illuminated by the headlights of police cars and emergency vehicles, the fir trees a peculiar light green against the night sky. Will could still smell the fire; he thought he could hear it, but people's voices and police radios and the noise of equipment were getting all mixed up in his head.

He tried to find Sam and saw, next to his parents, Mrs. MacDowell clinging to her husband's arm. Mr. MacDowell's voice shook as he said to Henry Wyeth, "I don't know how we can ever thank you."

"I just thank God that they're alive," the fleet owner replied.

Will stared at the man in disbelief. Wyeth looked back calmly and said, "We all should give thanks."

"You, especially, Henry."

The woman's raspy voice silenced the crowd. Will heard metal tags dangling behind him, then felt a dog's nose against his ear. It was Old Gold.

Olivia Winters stepped forward. "You should get down on your knees and give thanks that you're not being charged with manslaughter."

Will slid his arm around the golden retriever's neck. The dog steadied him.

"What bee's in your britch this time, Olivia?" Mr. Wyeth challenged.

"Come now, Henry. Everyone here knows you own this land. They may be interested to know I bought the house—with the petty cash you paid for my father's and brother's boats.

"It was hard on you, I'm sure, to discover your prime rental property could not be built on while the house still remained. It wasn't very nice of young Mr. May not to tell you that.

"But that was your mistake. You should have listened to your gran when she told shore stories. Oh, I know, you were never much interested in the past—in an old tale like the one about a will that split apart a family."

"Get to your point, Olivia."

"You must have been miffed when you found out you couldn't build. You must have felt a little desperate."

"Are you saying Henry Wyeth set this fire?" someone asked.

"And the other two as well," Toes announced boldly. "He was trying to cover himself."

The fleet owner spun around.

"He wanted everyone to think *he* was a victim, too."

Will started to laugh, but tears stung his eyes at the same time, and he hid his face in the dog's thick coat.

"We can show you the flammable rags that Toes removed from the house earlier this evening," Edward volunteered. "And some matchbooks that may have Mr. Wyeth's fingerprints on them."

"Count on me, Henry, for other charges," Olivia said. "Harassment inside the house, the day you surprised me. Your man's attempt to kill my dog"— her voice grew quieter—"got the boy's instead."

Will clung to Old Gold.

"And I've evidence to add to the young lady's," she continued. "Peter—"

"Peter!" Mr. Wyeth exclaimed.

"Was more heartsick than homesick when he figured you out. Came to me scared witless—didn't know how to protect these kids from your nastiness."

Will began to sob. He could hear reports being radioed in. More police dispatched. The house almost gone. The firefighters concerned only with keeping the pine wood wetted down.

Someone lay a hand on his back. "Are you okay?" It was Sam's voice. "Will, are you okay?"

Will let go of Old Gold, but was too embarrassed to speak.

"I feel bad for you, Will, real bad about the house."

When Will looked up, his friend's eyes were pink.

After a moment, Sam said, "I think—we're okay."